FALLING *for the* BILLIONAIRE WOLF *and* HIS BABY

BLOOD MOON BROTHERHOOD

FALLING *for the* BILLIONAIRE WOLF *and* HIS BABY

BLOOD MOON BROTHERHOOD

USA TODAY BESTSELLING AUTHOR

SASHA A. SUMMERS

Entangled Publishing, LLC
644 Shrewsbury Commons Ave
STE 181
Shrewsbury, PA 17361
rights@entangledpublishing.com

Amara is an imprint of Entangled Publishing, LLC.

Edited by Candace Havens
Cover design by Kelly Martin
Cover photography by Marko_Marcello/BigStock
Shukaylova Zinaida, Lora liu, /Shutterstock

Manufactured in the United States of America

First Edition April 2017

Previously released on Entangled's Covet imprint

Chapter One

"Congratulations, you're the father." Hollis sounded like he was announcing time of death, not the birth of a child.

Finn stared blindly out the window, anger and frustration warring with utter disbelief. "You're sure?" He couldn't keep the razor-sharp edge from his voice. Hollis was just the messenger—one of the few people Finn could trust, one of the few that stood by him no matter what. *He* was the asshole who knocked up a long-forgotten one-night stand. *How* was the question. He was always careful. Extra careful when it came to sex. He had to be. "I met her four months ago, Hollis. Are you sure?" His grip on the phone tightened.

"I'm sure it's *yours*. A full-term, healthy baby. I can't guarantee much more." Hollis's voice remained calm, almost detached, as always. "Cara didn't make it. She has no family, no one to challenge custody of the baby."

Cara. She'd been so full of life, so hungry for the next big adventure. What they'd shared had been fast and furious. When they'd parted, it had been on good terms, no expectations or regrets. How could she be dead?

Hollis's words grabbed his attention. "Looking at the body—I'm not sure what happened."

"So, not a car accident?" Finn had wondered. Guilt and sadness kicked him in the gut.

"That would be the easy explanation. One that will be her official cause of death."

"But?"

"But I think there's more to it." Hollis sighed. "There's always more to it when we are involved. I'm going to have a look at her records, see what needs to be taken care of. I hate to point this out but…this isn't going to go over well with the others."

"No shit," Finn growled. "It's not exactly making my day, either." Hollis hadn't said it, but Finn knew the truth. Cara's death was on him. His fucking fault.

"No, I don't imagine it is." He paused, the silence loaded until he added, "As unfortunate as that is, he can't stay here."

"He?" Finn repeated, his brain already assessing damage control.

"Your son," Hollis finally snapped. "This is dangerous, Finn."

Because there was nobody or nothing like his…son. This boy could jeopardize everything they'd been striving for the last ten years. Words wouldn't come. His son. He might be a baby now, but what the hell would he become? What would he be capable of? Self-loathing, hot and bitter, flooded Finn's mouth.

"Jesus, Finn, are you listening?" Hollis paused. "He can't stay in the hospital. I've been handling tests, all his bloodwork, but I can't be here twenty-four seven. You must come get him. He's your responsibility."

Hollis was right. And there wasn't a single thing he could do about it. "Fine." The word was clipped.

"Today," Hollis added.

Meaning Finn needed to work faster on finding help. The initial call from Cara's agent the night before had given him a heads-up, but he'd known the kid wasn't his. It had been too soon, an impossibility. Now… He ran a hand through his hair, wanting to hit something. "Give me 'til noon. I'll be there." He sat in his tall-backed leather chair, slammed the phone onto the desk, and pressed his fingers to his temples.

What the fuck was he supposed to do? Babies weren't dogs—you couldn't put them in a kennel for the day. He wasn't equipped for this. His assistant, Marjorie, had pulled employee files for him last night—right before she'd quit. And this time, he didn't think she was coming back.

He'd met with two of the three assistants he deemed acceptable this morning. Neither was suitable. Nor did they act as if they could deal with the sort of *surprises* that might come with this baby. Contestant number three was his only hope. It's not like he could just call a nanny service, not yet. He'd have to wait a month. If this baby… He sighed, rolling his head and easing the tension in his neck.

Hollis was right—this was dangerous for them. Too many unknowns, too many variables, to turn over to a stranger.

Not to mention the Others. They would not be happy about this new addition. What they did about it was the real question. All he could do was wait. And that wasn't how he rolled.

The intercom beeped. "Mr. Regatti and Mr. Martin are here," the receptionist announced.

"Fine." He had a business to run, several million-dollar companies, to be exact. People counted on him. This would wait until noon. "I'll be in the conference room in five minutes. I need a pot of coffee."

"Yes, Mr. Dean," she answered, clicking off.

Regatti and Martin were all about projections and forecasts. They were his *advisors*, the best in their field, the best at keeping him on the strongest financial path. Which meant they'd give him shit about his choices—like always—and he'd do whatever he wanted—like always. He valued their input, but his instincts had the final say-so. And while he respected their relentless pursuit of solid numbers, it was going to be one hell of a long meeting.

He stood, slipped into his jacket, and adjusted the cufflinks of his shirt, putting thoughts of everything non-work related out of his mind.

Regatti wasn't thrilled with the numbers on the new hybrid sportster launch, wanted to re-eval the marketing plan and spend more time on foreign markets.

Martin had a shit-fit over the money he was sinking into Robbin Pharmaceuticals & Research. They believed RPR was a lost cause, neither spearheading nor manufacturing anything that wasn't already available on the market. Finn knew the truth. Hollis Robbins's research was invaluable, to the masses and to a very specific population he had a personal interest in. Dean's investment was non-negotiable, and he made that clear.

When they left, neither was happy.

Finn glanced at his watch. Ten thirty. His irritation returned with a vengeance. He could only hope Jessa Talbot was the right one for the assistant job. He didn't have time to find someone else. But his preliminary reading, and Brown's thorough background check, had suggested she was the most likely candidate. Educated, well-liked, with excellent references and reviews. According to Brown, no one had a negative thing to say about the woman. But two key things stood out to Finn: Jessa Talbot was the primary caregiver to four younger siblings, and she was struggling financially—desperately. Meaning Miss Talbot had hands-on experience and compelling motivation to accept his offer.

He strode into the waiting room of his office, tense and

wary. A new scent reached him, sending his senses on high alert. He scanned the room, his attention locking on a woman staring out the floor to ceiling window.

Long blond hair twisted into a knot with a pencil stuck through.

The collar of her white shirt was worn, but the garment was pressed and clean.

Black skirt that hugged an amazing ass and killer legs.

Her pulse was rapid—agitated. There was a slight waver to her breath. He listened, far too intrigued. He closed his eyes, reining in the purely primal response she stirred.

The silver chain he wore beneath his dress shirt felt hot and heavy, the instincts he fought against daily rising in challenge. His wolf was waiting, demanding to know who she was. But deep inside Finn wasn't sure he liked the answer.

• • •

"Close the door, please." Finnegan Dean's voice was low, warm, but hardly comforting. She swallowed, hoping he couldn't see how completely rattled she was by this abrupt summons. "Miss Talbot?"

Jessa closed the carved wooden door, drawing in a long, slow breath to settle the anxiety tightening her throat. It wasn't every day she was called to Finnegan Dean's office. As the head of Dean Industries, time was a precious thing. Invariably, she worst-cased things.

Was she getting fired? Her siblings' future relied on her staying employed. Shelby and Harry's tuition was coming due, and Landon's college application fees were starting to roll in. Had she done something wrong? Yes, she'd come in late a few days, but she'd always made up for it—missing lunches or staying long into the night. She flexed her hands, smoothing her clammy palms along the seams of her fitted black pencil skirt. Surely not. It didn't make sense. After three years of sterling employee evaluations, he had to know she gave her all to his company. She could not lose this job. She turned, assuming as calm a demeanor as possible.

Finnegan Dean waited, his bright gaze steady, piercing—unapologetically intense. The longer he stared at her, the more concerned she became. His expression was blank, only the firm tick of his jaw muscle revealed stress. When his gaze returned to the papers on his desk, she could breathe again.

"Please, sit," his voice remained low, his attention never wandering from the document he was reading.

Jessa sat in one the large leather chairs opposite his heavy carved desk, feeling small and invisible. She tried not to stare at the man before her. He looked like a model. One of those ridiculously perfect-looking men. From a cologne ad, maybe. Perfect, chiseled profile. Clear, blue eyes. Dark blonde hair, tousled just so. He was big and broad—undoubtedly muscled and fit underneath his impeccably tailored suit—shrinking the room.

She stared at her hands, clasped tightly in her lap. But the agitated rhythm his long, tapered fingers tapped out on his desktop drew her attention back to him. Whatever he was reading, he seemed engrossed. His eyes narrowed briefly, the soft tapping stopped, and his brow arched. But then his features eased and he set the paper aside.

Cool, assessing eyes regarded her as he propped his elbow on the edge of the desk and rested his chin on his fist. Jessa prepared for the worst, every muscle tensing in anticipation. But, in a company this size, surely Mr. Dean wouldn't summon her into his office just to fire her.

"How are you, Miss Talbot?" He paused. "Do you enjoy your work as Miss Ramirez's executive assistant?"

She shifted in the chair, considering his questions. Miss Ramirez? Was this for her review? How to put it nicely?

Eileen Ramirez wasn't the worst boss she'd had, but Jessa would be hard pressed to say much positive about her current supervisor. It was a job. A job that paid well. A job she could not afford to lose. "I'm well, Mr. Dean. I'm very happy working here and being part of Dean Industries. Thank you."

There. That was a safe answer.

From the tightening of his mouth and the narrowing of his brilliant blue eyes, he knew it, too.

He sat back in his chair. "I'll be blunt, Miss Talbot. I'm creating a new opening to be filled immediately. I need someone on the inside, someone I can trust with every facet of my life, no questions asked. Someone capable of troubleshooting in even the most... *unusual* of situations." Tension rolled off the man in waves. "With absolute discretion, of course."

She blinked, her fear evaporating. A new position. Was he referring to Miss Ramirez? Or... She swallowed, carefully holding her enthusiasm in check while asking, "Is this...is this an interview, Mr. Dean?"

"Possibly." His attention wandered back to the file on his desk. "I'd like to discuss your résumé. Your bachelor's degree was in education? And much of your work during and before college was in educational settings?"

She nodded, confused by this line of questioning. "I'd planned on becoming a teacher."

"But then you went on to get your MBA?"

"I needed to be able to provide for my family. The wage disparity for teachers—"

"Is deplorable, yes." He paused, rubbing his chin with his knuckles. "Let me stress that this is a highly sensitive... project. It runs approximately six weeks. In that time, I own you. You will eat, breathe, and sleep work." His blue gaze swept her face. "You've dealt with some of my most... challenging employees and managed to come out unscathed. Your reviews are exceptional, mentioning your ability to think on your feet, take charge, and work tirelessly to ensure best results." He read aloud.

I own you. She swallowed, trying not to be distracted by the gravel in his voice. He was talking about a new job, reporting directly to him. Nothing more. And yet, his voice unleashed something molten in the base of her stomach. She cleared her throat, stiffening her posture. "May I ask a question?"

"Of course." He tapped his pen.

"You said six weeks. After that, what happens?" She waited.

He paused, watching her—closely. The hair on the back of her neck stood up. His eyes traveled over her face, lingered on her neck, then swept up to her eyes once more. He cleared his throat before going on. "Once this project is over, you will stay on with me as my executive assistant. If nothing else, this project will ensure we are compatible. My assistants need to be organized, focused—someone I can call on day and night." His smile was slow—and lethal. "I'm not going to lie to you—I'm a pain in the ass to work for. But I believe in promoting from within and, obviously, this would give you the opportunity to show me what you have to offer Dean Industries."

She smiled back then immediately regretted it.

His gaze sharpened, dropping to her mouth before locking with hers. "I believe this could benefit us both, Miss Talbot." He paused, shifting in his chair. "I know you've raised four younger siblings, as caregiver and primary provider. I also know that finances are tight."

She swallowed. How? She glanced at the papers spread across his desk. What else did he know? "We manage," her voice was tight. *Barely.* He had no idea how tiring it was. How many nights she'd crawl into bed wondering if they'd ever get ahead? If she'd ever stop worrying over their future. Or if she'd ever have a life of her own.

"It's safe to say you feel comfortable dealing with children? That you've experience with… babies?"

It was impossible to miss the scorn in his voice. She frowned. "Yes. My parents died when Nate, the youngest, was a few months old." Since their aunt hadn't been the hands-on, kid-friendly type, Jessa had been mother and sister.

He nodded and sighed heavily, pinching his nose and closing his eyes. "Then, I have two questions for you. Are you willing to put in the substantial extra hours required, in a non-traditional work environment? And can I count on your complete and total discretion?" He glanced at her. "To start, I'll double your salary and give you a bonus that should cover the next tuition payments for your brother and sister. I will also help your brothers gain admission to the schools they want. Staying there will be their responsibility."

Her heart was hammering, the prick of tears undeniable. This was a huge opportunity. He had no idea what this meant to her—to her family. She might not have to refinance the house. Any concerns over how vague he was being faded away. How could she say no? "Yes."

"Good. If you've been working on anything else, tell Mrs. Daugherty. She can take over."

She waited, hoping he'd provide more information. This project… Considering his line of questioning, it had something to do with children. Possibly an on-site daycare facility? Something that wouldn't fall within the parameters of his seemingly carefree, extravagant life—full of beautiful people and exotic adventures. At least, that's the way the papers portrayed him. To her, his life was all glamor and excitement—things that didn't exist in her world.

"May I ask about this project, Mr. Dean?"

His eyes slammed into her, searching… He seemed hesitant to tell her. "Apparently, I have a son."

He had a son? She wasn't sure what to say or how to react. Or what, exactly, that had to do with her...

"It's a surprise to me, too, let me assure you. We have a car to catch. I'll share the details on the way to the hospital." He ran a hand through his golden hair, a single curl falling onto his forehead.

"The hospital?" she asked, growing more perplexed.

"He was born yesterday morning," he clarified.

A million questions raced through her mind.

"Grab your things," he said. "I'll meet you in the lobby. We won't be returning to the office today."

She nodded, hurrying from his office and toward the elevators. She passed Lara, ignoring her friend's furious attempts to flag her down, and headed to her cubicle. In five minutes, she'd slipped into her coat, grabbed her bag, and was headed to the elevator, her questions settling into a more logical pattern. The one thing she wanted clarified: was his *son* her special project?

But seeing Finnegan Dean waiting for her in the lobby, cell phone to his ear, looking every bit the master of his domain, threw her off center again. His gaze swept over her, the slight furrow of his brows a question. She looked away, pretending to find the framed art in the lobby mesmerizing. She stood, waiting. His tone was no longer soft. No, each syllable dripped agitation. He glanced at her, nodded, and headed toward the front doors.

She hadn't expected him to wait for her, holding the door open, but he did, and she hurried through. When his hand rested on her lower back, Jessa shuddered. Electricity hummed up her spine, leaving her dazed. Being attracted to this man was a very bad thing. One she'd have to work on getting over.

Then his hand was gone, Mr. Dean's long strides putting distance between them.

She followed, trying to keep up in heels meant for walking, not jogging. A black car waited out front, the driver holding the back door wide. Mr. Dean climbed in, but Jessa hesitated, gripped with a sense of foreboding and uncertainty.

"Miss Talbot?" Mr. Dean's voice was tight, impatient.

She hurried forward, the driver offering her a slight smile as she climbed in behind Finnegan.

"I'll be there," he snapped. "Damage control is your job. A job you're paid very well to do."

A long silence fell over the car. She cast a quick glance his way. He was looking at her. Not her—her legs. She smoothed her hands over her skirt, tugging the fabric into place. His fingers tightened around his phone, and his gaze met hers. She folded her hands in her lap to hide their slight tremble.

"I need you to make sure there are no surprises," he finished, and hung up, still looking at her. But it was the *way* he was looking at her that was unnerving. She had a hard time breathing when his gaze bore into hers.

The car went over a bump, jolting Jessa and snapping her out of her daze and back to cool, calm, and professional. "Mr. Dean, I have questions," she began.

"I imagine you do." He nodded, a slight smile hovering on his lips—lips Jessa was far too distracted by.

She smoothed her skirt again, focusing on his eyes, not his mouth. His clear, pale blue eyes. "What will this job entail?"

"Preparing my house for an infant. Finding the right person to work as my son's nanny."

She drew in a deep breath. "The mother—"

"Died in childbirth." His voice was devoid of emotion.

"I'm sorry," she murmured.

His gaze left her, his attention focused on the view outside their window. "I didn't know her well."

She digested this news. His image was splashed across countless magazines and tabloids with a bevy of models, actresses, and debutantes. But he was rarely seen with the same woman for long. He'd earned the nickname "Speedster," a dig at both his dating style and his fondness for fast cars.

"Why not use an outside agency?" she asked.

"When I know my son has no special needs, I—you— will." He checked his watch, impatient. "Until then, you want a stable career and *need* financial security. You have a vested interest, one that ensures your complete discretion. I need someone I can trust implicitly."

She stared at him.

"I know nothing about children. Nothing. You, on the other hand, do." He glanced at his phone then pulled a file from his black leather bag. "To be blunt, I don't have time for this. I will do what I can to ensure *you* do the rest. I need to leave it in your capable hands—not worry about it. I also need your signature on these."

It? Project? So, Mr. Dean wasn't the paternal type. He'd suffered a shock and wasn't ready to accept his son yet. He would, in time—surely.

She scanned over the papers, processing the bizarre turn her morning had taken. A non-disclosure agreement? A man in his position would expect as much. In a sort of sad way, it made sense. She took the pen and signed the paper, then glanced out the window at the busy San Antonio streets. "A newborn is a lot of work—"

"As I said, six weeks. After that, you'll be relieved by the nanny selected."

She nodded, her suspicions confirmed. "Babies don't keep office hours."

His chuckle was soft—and far too delectable. "No, I don't suppose they do." He paused. "Your brothers are old enough to handle things for a short time?"

She nodded, the unexpected rasp of his chuckle rendering her speechless. Pathetic.

"Once we pick him up, we will stop to collect your things. This is for you," he said, handing her a cell phone. "My numbers, my housekeeper, and the driver's numbers are all programmed, as well as any alarm codes." He offered her a set of keys on a large gold ring, and a black charge card. "These are yours. Anything you need, use the card."

Day and night. With Finnegan Dean. She should be thrilled, not nervous. She took the keys and card, placing them in her purse. "What do you have for…him?"

He frowned. "Nothing."

She hesitated, her mind working ahead. "A car seat?" she asked.

He shook his head.

"They won't let us take him without a car seat," she argued.

His frown increased. "I'm sure they will—"

"No, Mr. Dean, it's the law," she assured him, trying not to smile. "The law is the law, even for you."

He laughed, surprising her. "Fine. A car seat. And where do we get a car seat?"

She smiled. "Two blocks up, on the left. They should have them at Klemp's Store."

Chapter Two

Finn watched Jessa Talbot read over the safety brochures attached to the infant car seats. Her scent had been damn-near crippling since she'd closed herself in his office. He'd hoped the dumpy, aging redhead in accounting had been Jessa Talbot. She definitely *wasn't*. His wolf was thrilled—and on the verge of taking control. Just his luck.

A distraction. A dangerous distraction.

He would never have hired this woman for that very reason.

It didn't matter how impressive her résumé was. Or how agreeable she was. She was a no-go zone. He couldn't afford to employ people who threatened his control. And something about her had very definitely put his wolf on high-alert.

Her scent didn't help. She smelled like heaven. Sweet. Feminine. Something that needed protection—from someone like him.

It didn't matter. Complicated or not, she was all he had. He needed her. That trumped everything else. Including the urge to push her into his bed and bury himself inside her. He wasn't an animal, no matter what the fuck the wolf thought. She was the person he—they—needed. Knowledge that eased some of the worry crushing him since Hollis's call.

A child was involved now. *His* son.

Hollis's warning still rang in his ears. *"When they find out about him, he's in danger. Real danger. We all are."*

"This is the one," Jessa said, patting the large, navy-blue monstrosity. "Best crash test ratings." She winced at the price tag. "It's a little pricey."

He reached for the tag, his fingers brushing hers. He bit back a hiss, glad she withdrew her hand so quickly. This was going to be difficult. Drowning in her scent was bad enough. But the thrill of awareness—almost recognition—touching her caused was something else. He'd have to be more careful. He focused on the now-bent tag he held, glanced at the price, then her. "Miss Talbot. You're buying for me now. This is not pricey."

She pressed her lips together.

"What?" he asked. Her lips were full and, undoubtedly, soft.

"Nothing," she argued.

"Say it," he pushed, enjoying the play of emotion on her face. She was very expressive.

"For the real world, this is pricey, Mr. Dean." She nodded at the car seat, smiling.

"Well, you're living in my world now," he said, amused—and irritated. She had no idea what that statement truly meant. His world was undoubtedly more like one of Jessa Talbot's nightmares. He needed to remember that where she was concerned.

He left her to check out then headed back to the car. Restlessness gripped him. Anger. Frustration. Impatience. He'd been careful. His life was a well-oiled, carefully constructed machine, with minimal to no hiccups. Every decision was analyzed, every outcome considered. Everything he did was premeditated, ensuring his secret was kept. No one would ever know what he was—what he'd done to his friends.

Hell, the only risks he'd taken the last ten years had been in business.

His personal life left no room for risks. No complications. No entanglements. No commitments. If he was attracted to a woman, he made sure they understood that and the inevitable outcome. Few turned him down. He'd met Cara four months ago; she'd been no different. They'd had a great week, lots of sex—*all* protected—and parted ways. And yet, somehow, she still ended up pregnant with his baby.

He was a father.

He had a baby. A son.

A fucking ticking time bomb.

The five of them had sworn this infection, as Hollis liked to call it, would end with them. Hollis. Dante. Anders. Malachi. And him. They had no way of predicting what their offspring would be, so kids, families, were off the table. None of them wanted anyone else getting hurt…

Anders would give him shit, but he'd laugh it off.

Dante's expression would say it all. It'd be hard to look him in the eye for a while.

Hollis was disappointed. But the man was a scientist first, and there was no denying he was excited to see Finnegan Dean's latest creation.

But Malachi. Mal hadn't said one word to him in nine years. This wouldn't change much. Unless Mal decided to come kick his ass. Finn wouldn't even fight back.

They needed to know. They had a right to know. This baby would impact them all.

As much as he valued his independence, he'd never felt so alone. He'd fucked up big. Again. Hollis was his answer man, and he didn't have any. *Only time would tell.*

How much time was another question.

But for now, this baby needed to be kept safe. Away from the world. Away from those that would see his existence as a threat. From those that would hunt him.

That's why he would put up with Jessa.

Why did her presence make his other side fight to take over? Some haywire instinct wanted her close—even though keeping her at arm's length was the right choice. She was the ultimate temptation for a man like him, and he'd just invited her home.

Fuck it.

Six weeks. He could do this. He would do this. He frowned. Temptation aside, instinct told him he could trust her. He'd have to hold on to that and hope the odd reaction his wolf was having would fade. Either way, when time was up, he'd find a place for her. One that kept her *far* from him. He had a London office, which might be the best option.

"Thomas needs to install it," Jessa was saying to him.

Who the hell was Thomas? He'd been blindly staring at his phone, so lost in his thoughts he'd missed her arrival. A store clerk stood holding the enormous car seat that would carry his baby son home. His name badge read THOMAS.

He'd been pacing, currently he was blocking the car door. He moved without a word, watching as the young man climbed in and walked Jessa through the safety features and how to ensure the seat was secure. She stooped, leaning in to see and hear. The view of her delectable backside snagged Finn's full attention.

The wolf wasn't the only one appreciating her lush hips, trim thighs, sculpted calves, all showcased by her fitted pencil skirt and heels. He closed his eyes, the thump of her heartbeat echoing in his ears. He listened, the primal thrill of connection sending his blood south and making him shove his hands in his pockets. He was rock hard, the zipper of his pants uncomfortable.

Jessa was off-limits. She had to be. For her safety.

She probably already had some adoring boyfriend that sent her flowers, remembered her birthdays, and enjoyed snuggling on the couch and watching movies with her. A normal guy, without full-moon phobias and the tendency to rip people to bits. *Lucky bastard.*

She stepped back, her heel catching in the sidewalk crack, and tipped backward. He moved, catching her. The crush of her curves against his straining erection had him biting off a curse. His hands tightened on her arms, ensuring she was safe. He held her, blindsided by the surge of ownership that tore through him. *Let her go*, he demanded of his wolf. He released her, sidestepping around her as the clerk climbed out of the car.

He avoided her stare, grappling with the rush still coursing through his body. What the fuck was that? He didn't know. He didn't want to know. Ignoring her, ignoring *this*, was the right choice.

"That should do it. If you have questions, you can call me." Thomas's tone was a little too friendly for Finn's liking. Clearly, Thomas wasn't immune to Jessa's charms. And he had no problem being obvious about it, either. "And if I can help you with anything else, you know where to find me. Anytime."

Finn shot the young man a look. "We need to go," he said.

"Yes, of course," she agreed, hurrying around to get into the car.

Get a fucking grip. This was not the time to get territorial. He rested his head on the seat back until the roaring pulse in his veins eased. Only then did he risk glancing at her. If he wasn't careful, she'd walk, money or not, which was something he couldn't risk. He needed to keep his shit together. If he was lucky, she'd never learn what he or his son were. Jessa Talbot was an essential employee—nothing more. She seemed to be inventorying the contents of the large bag at her feet. His eyes traveled over her profile, the curve of her nose, the length of her neck. A beautiful essential employee. And her pulse, her breathing… Was she aware of him? Or was she simply anxious from all the changes the last thirty minutes had delivered? *Dammit.* "Supplies?" he asked, breaking the silence.

"I tried to be quick. Diapers," she said, peering into the bag. "And wipes. Some bottles, infant formula, a few gowns and blankets. This won't last long."

"I imagine you could call Thomas and he would deliver?" he asked, sounding far too condescending.

She turned, regarding him with bright green eyes. "Probably."

"Good." He cleared his throat and pulled his phone from his pocket. "Make a list, call him, and have it delivered." He answered emails, checked stocks, anything to prevent staring at her.

The rest of the drive was silent. The closer they got to the hospital, the thicker the tension became. He wasn't angry; there was no reason to be angry. He was on edge because of the whole situation. Not because he couldn't have a normal life. Be a normal man. Have a normal relationship. He understood those things, accepted them. But right now, the weight of shit he shouldered seemed heavier than usual. Unease knotted his stomach.

He was hyperaware of his surroundings as they entered the hospital. The heat and crush of people. The myriad hum of voices and machines. The lingering smell of blood and bleach. He took it all in, every sense on high alert, braced, ready. By the time they climbed onto the elevator, his heart was thundering.

"Are you all right?" Jessa asked. Her eyes radiated concern—true sympathy. The gentle pressure of her hand on his arm was oddly soothing, for him and the beast inside. He wanted to draw her closer, touch her. He didn't. He stared at her hand and drew in a deep breath. "I think so."

She squeezed lightly, then seemed to realize she was touching him. She lifted her hand and smiled. "My aunt used to say life only gives us what we can handle."

"I'm not sure I agree. I'm not handling this, you are." Her aunt had no idea. His attention wandered to her throat, the slight thrum of her pulse. He closed his eyes, letting her even heartbeat steady him, her scent fill him.

"This?" she asked. "A baby? There's not much mystery to them. They cry, sleep, and eat."

He studied her face, admiring her confidence. "Perhaps I have a few things in common with my son."

She laughed.

The doors opened and the two of them walked to the nurse's desk. After that, things blurred together. The hospital room. The nurse giving Jessa papers, talking and talking. Words that made no sense. A metal cart rolling into the room. The flutter of a heartbeat, the rapid, shallow breathing of the infant inside. But it was the scent that spoke the truth.

He wasn't prepared for the tidal wave of emotion that engulfed him. He, Finnegan Dean, was a monster.

Now he was a father.

He had a son.

The first-born werewolf of his reluctant pack.

• • •

Jessa stared around the large bedroom, the magnitude of the last few hours registering. She was in Finnegan Dean's house. She was *moving into* Finnegan Dean's house. And, no matter how hard she wanted to deny it, something about the man fascinated her. No, "fascinated" wasn't strong enough.

This is bad.

She glanced at the clock on the wall. After the enormity of the morning, it seemed impossible that it was only three o'clock. Once they'd left the hospital, Mr. Dean had offered to stop to get her things, but she hadn't wanted to keep Oscar out in the cold any longer than necessary. Her brother Harry was bringing over a bag of her things around five—not that he was happy about it. She'd tried to explain the situation but thought it would be easier to do so face-to-face. Without Mr. Dean within earshot of the conversation.

A soft squeak on the bed made her turn.

Oscar. Oscar Finnegan Dean the Fourth to be precise. A precious baby boy, sound asleep on her bed. This little guy was her responsibility.

A responsibility that gave her a new life. No more Miss Ramirez. No heels. No office politics. For now. Late night feedings and diaper changes were nothing. It was more like a six-week vacation.

A vacation in a swanky hotel.

A vacation with a man who seemed to have a direct line to her nervous system. Everything about him set off a current, white-hot, startling, and throbbing. He'd headed for the office after showing her around, but he'd be back eventually. She needed to figure out how to control her response to him—or cut the connection altogether. This job was just too important.

Her room looked like something out of an architecture and design magazine. Bold finishes. Modern fixtures. Muted colors. Even with a king-size bed, a desk, and a chaise before the large floor-to-ceiling picture windows, her room felt almost empty.

As impressive as the space was, it didn't radiate warmth. Or home. Or happiness. She glanced at the sleeping baby and smiled. "Not that you'll notice for a while." Oscar's mouth nursing, his little fingers splayed, then clenched as he slept on. He was perfect.

She tucked the blanket around him and padded barefoot across the room. Staring down through the window, she could see the busy streets below, the traffic and pedestrians of downtown San Antonio steady. The rest of the world hadn't changed—even if hers had.

But she still had work to do.

She settled at her desk, opened the laptop already set up, and pulled out the suggested supply list from the hospital. She searched for Klemp's site online and started shopping. Before she hit buy, she picked up her new phone and called. Thomas guaranteed delivery within the next few hours.

Once that was done, she sat on the bed by Oscar. He was beautiful. She'd only held him long enough to move him from the bassinette to his car seat, but his slight weight and baby smell had tugged something deep inside of her. He'd made an adorable gurgle, sighed, and settled into an easy sleep. She'd tucked the thick blanket she'd purchased around him and stood back, but Mr. Dean hadn't offered to carry him.

In fact, Mr. Dean hadn't offered to touch his son. He'd barely looked at him.

"It's okay, Oscar, your daddy will figure it out soon enough," she said, stroking the baby's cheek. "Sometimes grown-ups take a while to adjust to changes. And, tiny as you are, you're a huge change for someone like your father."

Oscar grunted, wiggled, and burst into tears.

She grinned and picked him up. She cradled him close, once more appreciating just how tiny he was. "Are you tired of lying there?" she asked. "Well, let's get you changed and something to eat."

She'd unloaded her bag from Klemps earlier, prepared for the eventual end of Oscar's nap. She changed his diaper, inspecting his toes and fingers, his long legs, a birthmark on his little hip, and rounded tummy. He was perfect—and red-faced and screaming by the time he was swaddled and cradled against her chest.

"Come on," she said, unruffled. "Let's get you something to eat, shall we?"

Mr. Dean's housekeeper, Augustina, wasn't the least bit pleased with Jessa or Oscar's arrival. And since she had no idea what Mr. Dean had said to the woman by way of introduction, she could do little but make small talk and act like nothing was out of the ordinary.

She smiled at the middle-aged woman as she made Oscar's bottle, chatting to the baby the whole time. She'd always done that; her mother had told her the best thing she could do with her brothers was talk to them and let them hear her voice. It made them feel less afraid and alone—or so her mother had said.

Once the formula was ready, Jessa cradled Oscar and offered him the bottle.

"He's loud," Augustina said.

"He is," Jessa agreed.

"There's a rocking chair in the front room," Augustina said, pointing. "Through there."

"Thank you." Jessa left, carefully cuddling Oscar as she headed down the hall and into the front room. It was as modern as the rest of the house. Impressive, but stark. The rocking chair resembled a piece of modern art but was surprisingly comfortable. She sat, bracing Oscar on her shoulder to burp him. He did, with gusto.

"Well, that was impressive," she said, laughing.

She looked up to find Finnegan Dean standing in the doorway. He was watching them curiously, frozen in place. "It was," he agreed.

Oscar fussed then, so Jessa offered him the rest of the bottle. "Would you like to feed him, Mr. Dean?"

"No," he said, his gaze intense.

She turned her focus back to the baby then. If Oscar

Finnegan Dean the third wasn't ready to accept Oscar Finnegan Dean the fourth, then she'd have to compensate for it. *At least for now*.

"Did you shop?" he asked.

"Yes. Thomas said everything would arrive by five," she said.

"I'm sure he did," he said softly. "Anytime now."

She nodded. "Which room is Oscar's?"

"The one next to yours," he said. "I'll have it emptied." He typed something on his phone. "What else?"

She shook her head. "Do you have any requirements you'd like the nanny agency to consider? I know it's early, but I want to contact them now, give them time to pull the best candidates versus waiting until the last minute."

"Experience and length of service with each family." He leaned against the doorframe, looking at the baby in her arms. "I don't want him to get attached to someone who will leave him."

She nodded, glancing at Oscar. He was dozing, his little pink lips sliding off the bottle. She smiled, lifted him against her shoulder, and patted his back.

"No one under forty. I don't want anyone hoping to get to me through him," he added.

She looked at Finnegan Dean, struggling to understand the position he was in. He was a wealthy, gorgeous man. Of course women would use any angle available to try to win him over. What would that be like, to be so sought after? To be wary and suspect of everyone you met? Clearly he didn't feel that way about her. She didn't know if that was a compliment...or an insult. She decided to believe the former.

"I'll do my best, Mr. Dean." She stood, walking closer. "He has long legs and a birthmark on his hip."

"Does he... Ten fingers and toes?" He stared at the baby with...fear?

Poor Finnegan Dean. She smiled. "He's perfect. Would you like to hold him?"

"No." His gaze moved to her then. "Not yet."

She nodded, gripped with sympathy. She was still processing the changes in her day, but this wasn't her life. In six weeks, her life would return to normal—for the most part. But Mr. Dean would come home to his son every night until the day little Oscar went off to college. A daunting change for a man used to freedom.

She shifted Oscar in her arms, his little hand catching the silk neckline of her blouse and pulling the fabric down. The lace edge of her pale pink bra was a stark contrast to her dark gray blouse. She lifted his tiny hand and tucked it into his blanket, her cheeks hot as she tried to adjust her clothing.

She glanced at Mr. Dean, hoping he'd missed the whole slip. He stood, his eyes pressed tightly closed and his brow furrowed deeply.

The doorman buzzed, and Mr. Dean's eyes opened, his gaze slipping over her. "Thomas," he murmured.

"Or Harry," she offered, hurrying to explain Harry's no-doubt irritated attitude. "He's not thrilled that he'll be in charge. If he's a bit prickly, that's why."

"I'll keep that in mind." Mr. Dean smiled, pressing the button by the intercom. "Yes?"

"A large delivery sir," the doorman said.

Oscar chose that moment to burp then dissolved into tears. She patted him, bouncing him gently in her arms, while Finnegan Dean stared in horror. She carried the baby out, knowing Oscar's screams were hard to talk over. She kept bouncing and patting, making her way to her room. Once there, she changed Oscar into a dry diaper and wrapped him in a clean blanket before scooping him up and walking toward the window.

He calmed, grunting and wriggling until he was

comfortable enough to fall back to sleep.

She spread another blanket on the middle of the bed and laid Oscar on his back, surrounding him with pillows for her benefit. He was too little to roll, she knew that. She waited, one hand resting on his swaddled body, to ensure he was sleeping peacefully. He didn't stir, but his little mouth suckled in his sleep, and she stood. She smiled, left the door ajar, and made her way down the hall.

"Hey, Jessa," Thomas said, waiting. "You want to check over the list and make sure we have everything you requested?"

She took the clipboard from him, checking off each item before signing off. "I appreciate how prompt you were."

"If you point me in the right direction, I'll assemble the crib before I go," he offered.

She led him down the hall to the room that adjoined hers through a shared bathroom. It was a large, airy room with a wonderful view of the new park. She could imagine a window seat with pillows piled high and a tower of books to read.

"I think it will fit here," she said.

He nodded.

"Do you need anything?" she asked.

"I brought my own tools." He smiled, looking at her with an appreciative eye.

"I'll leave you to it," she said, turning to go...and found Mr. Dean watching them. "This is Oscar's room? It's perfect, lots of room to grow." She smiled at him. "Thomas has offered to assemble the crib."

"Good," Mr. Dean said. "I have a conference call soon. I'll be unavailable for some time."

She nodded. She understood why he was here, working from home, and that today was one distraction after another. Not his norm. He was usually at the office late. Lara, the fifth-floor receptionist and her frequent lunch buddy, lived to tell her all about Finnegan Dean's comings and goings. And, per Lara, Mr. Dean was a schedule man. "I'll try to keep things quiet."

He nodded, glanced at Thomas, and left.

"Your boss is pretty intense," Thomas said once they were alone. "But I love Dean Automotive cars. Some of the few cars on the road that still have a unique profile."

She nodded. "You can spot a Dean vehicle a mile away."

"Good company to work for?" Thomas asked, opening the box and pulling out the pieces.

"Definitely," she agreed.

"So, Jessa, what do you do after hours?" he asked, smiling.

She smiled back. "I go home to three younger brothers. And a sister, though she's out of state—at college. Never a dull moment in my house."

"Three?" He frowned. "They have to approve your dates?"

She laughed. "I don't date very often."

"I'd like to change that," he said. "Maybe, if you're free, you'd consider having dinner with me?"

He *was* nice. And handsome. The kind of guy that would be easy to fall into a relationship with. Maybe she should give it a try. It had been two years since she broke up with Benjamin. And there were times she forgot she was a young woman with every right to a social life.

"When would this dinner date be?" she asked. "I'm on call for…a while." Six weeks sounded like a put-off, and she didn't want him to think she wasn't interested. He was definite maybe.

"After a while sounds good," he said, smiling. "Since I'm thinking you'll be needing more baby supplies in the meantime?"

"Probably," she agreed.

He nodded, leveling her with a look of pure masculine

appreciation.

She heard the intercom buzzer and hurried from the room. "Yes?"

"Miss Talbot? There's a Mr. Harry Talbot here to see you?" the doorman's voice crackled.

"Please send him up," she said, pressing the button.

Five minutes later, Harry arrived. His confusion was almost comical.

"What's going on?" he asked, lugging her large suitcase behind him. "You're shacking up with your boss?"

She rolled her eyes. "Really, Harry? I'm not shacking up with anyone." She took the smaller suitcase from him and led him down the hall to her room. "I *am* helping Mr. Dean out for a while," she explained. "Did you bring everything I asked?"

He followed her into her room. "I hope so. Nice digs," he said. "This is only for a couple of weeks, right?"

"Maybe more." She nodded, intentionally vague to prevent full-blown panic on the home front. She and Oscar would be making regular visits; she was certain of that. "You found the schedule I emailed? There are plenty of casseroles in the freezer to last a while. Do *not* order pizza every night."

Harry sighed.

"I mean it," she continued. "Pizza is expensive and, unless you get a second job, an extravagance we can't afford."

"I know," he said. "This the rug rat?" he asked, looking at Oscar sleeping on the bed. "He's cute. Super new, from the looks of him."

"This is Oscar," she said. Oscar kept right on snoozing, making her smile. "Oscar, this is Harry, my little brother."

"He's thrilled to meet me," Harry said.

"Everyone's thrilled to meet you, Harry." She hugged her brother. "Promise me you'll keep everything on track."

"Jessa, I am about to graduate from college. I think I can make sure the others don't burn down the house for a week—"

"And make sure homework gets done. If you don't check it, it's not done. Trust me on this," she added. "And make sure Nate takes his asthma meds and gets to his guitar lesson."

"And has karate on Tuesday, I know," he said, sounding exasperated.

"Okay, fine, I'll lay off," she said.

Harry laughed. "That'll be a first."

She laughed, too. "Smart-ass."

"So all the stuff piled in the hallway is for him?" Harry asked. "How does something so little need so much?"

"I was wondering the same thing," Mr. Dean said, joining them. "But I trust your sister's judgement entirely. Finnegan Dean," he said, offering his hand. "You must be Harry?"

Harry shook his hand. "Nice to meet you, Mr. Dean."

"Finn, please," Mr. Dean said.

"Finn," Harry repeated. "My sister is all-knowing when it comes to kids—plenty of experience. And she's frugal. So, if she bought it, she must think you need it."

She smiled. "You're being nice."

Harry grinned. "I didn't think you'd appreciate me calling you a tightwad in front of your boss."

Finnegan Dean laughed. "I appreciate someone watching my overhead expenses for me."

She glanced at Mr. Dean, more than a little stunned by just how beautiful he was when he laughed, then her brother. "Feeding three teenage boys is all about watching expenses. So, remember, there are plenty of casseroles in the freezer. You will not starve, no matter what the others might say."

"I got it, I got it," Harry said, holding up his hands.

She frowned at him. "We'll see how long you go before you call me."

"Why not write up a list, and I'll have it delivered," Mr. Dean offered.

"You don't have to," she assured him.

"It's no trouble. Considering the inconvenience I've caused your family," he continued.

She tried again, "No inconvenience—"

"I insist, Miss Talbot." His tone was authoritative, ending her arguments and giving rise to a slight flare of irritation.

"Just call this number and tell them what you want when you need it. No questions asked." He handed Harry a card.

Harry glanced at her, reluctant, before tucking the card into his pocket. "Thank you. Guess I should head out, make sure homework is getting done and the house isn't in a state of emergency." He winked at her, dropping a kiss on her cheek. "Don't worry, Jessa. We can behave."

She arched a brow. "When you want to."

"Mr. Dean—Finn." Harry nodded at Finn.

"Nice to meet you, Harry," he said. "I'll walk you out."

She tried to dismiss her irritation. She had a hard time taking help from others. Most of her life had been about becoming self-sufficient. And while Finnegan Dean might think nothing of his offer, it was no small thing to her.

She unpacked the infant monitor and put in batteries, then cut off tags and set Oscar's new clothing aside to wash. She'd prefer to wash everything before using them on Oscar, to ensure the he didn't have allergies.

She glanced at the baby, still sleeping, and smiled. So little and helpless. She could only imagine the life this boy would have, the experiences and adventures he'd live. Travel, the best education, and wealth…. And, right now, it was up to her to find the best person to love him—other than his father.

She sat on the bed, placing a hand on the baby boy. "Don't you worry, Oscar. I'll find you the best nanny. She'll give you kisses and hugs, and twirl you around. She'll sing to you and read with you and play pretend and let you make messes. You can count on me."

Chapter Three

Finnegan stood outside her door, frozen. *You can count on me.* She meant it, he heard it in her voice.

That wasn't something he'd heard a lot of growing up. If anything, his parents' absence was the one thing he could count on. How many nannies had he and his brother gone through in their youth? Not that he and Philip had ever given them a reason to stick around. They were too eager to put tacks in their nannies' chairs and hemorrhoid cream in place of their toothpaste. They were relentless. So much so, their parents had divided them up, sending them to boarding schools on opposite sides of the country. By the time they'd reached college, they were different people—never as close as they were. Then Philip met Annie, and Finn had been infected. Being close to anyone was no longer an option.

You can count on me.

Jessa's humming reached him, soft and sweet. Just like she was. Exactly what he wanted for his son. Oscar deserved that—to have someone read and sing and laugh with him. To love him unconditionally. He didn't know how to do that, how to let anyone close. The risk was too great.

He turned on his heel and headed back across the apartment. Why the hell had he come home early to begin with? There was enough work to keep him occupied at the office, away from the distractions.

Yet, he couldn't stay away.

The need to be close to Oscar was overwhelming. The wolf needed it, he needed it. Less than two hours after leaving them at the apartment, he was back.

As Oscar was being cradled close by Jessa, he had a phone call to make. Time to let the others know what had happened. He owed them that. Hell, he owed them a hell of a lot more. He pushed his office door closed, lifted the handle of the old-fashioned landline phone, and started punching in numbers.

"You ready?" Hollis asked.

"No," Finn admitted. "But waiting won't make it easier."

"It won't," Hollis agreed.

Anders and Dante answered, but Malachi went straight to voicemail.

"Did you really think he'd answer?" Dante asked.

"I hoped," Finn said.

"So what's going on? I've been goose-pimpled out all day," Anders's connection was patchy—his cabin was in the middle of nowhere and nothing.

"I have a son." Finn figured ripping off the Band-Aid was better than dragging it out. "We have a new…"

"I thought puppies were off the table?" Anders asked.

"Jesus, Finn," Dante groaned. "Did you forget how to use a condom? The instructions are right there on the frigging box."

"I was careful, dammit. I'm always careful. Guess it didn't work." They had every right to be upset. He went on, "He's here. No changing it."

"Just one?" Anders asked. "So, we don't have litters?

Man, that's a relief." He chuckled.

"Just one," Hollis joined in. "He appears, for the time being, human."

The line was silent.

"Human?" Anders asked. "So, no wet nose and wagging tail?"

"Are you saying we won't pass this on?" Dante asked.

"I'm not saying that," Hollis said. "But, for now, there's no indication that Oscar will suffer from our affliction."

"You mean he's not a werewolf?" Dante pushed.

"Not yet," Hollis said. "Maybe never."

"Then why were my Spidey-senses tingling?" Anders asked.

Dante sighed. "Yeah, I knew something was up, too."

Just like Finn had known Oscar was his. The bond was there, instantaneously. As much as he wanted to believe Hollis was right, he knew the truth. His voice was thick, his throat tight, as he murmured, "He's one of us."

"Shit," Dante groaned.

"What's happened?" Hollis asked.

"I…I know he's mine. I feel it—that connection we have. Only stronger." Finn sat down in his chair and rested his head on the headrest.

"So, in three weeks, what happens?" Anders asked. "We gonna have some mini-wolf running around chewing up the city?"

"Three weeks…" A full moon meant taking Oscar someplace safe. "I'll take him to the reserve. Safest there."

"I'll meet you there," Hollis said.

"Me, too," Anders offered. "Be good to have a change of pace. Meet the little guy."

"Well, shit, guess I have to come, too," Dante said. "Since we don't know what's going to happen."

"I'd advise against it. You know the Others can track us

easier when we're together. Just because they know Finn is alpha doesn't mean they know you two exist." Hollis's no-nonsense response earned a snort from Anders and silence from Dante.

"He's right. Mal and I are known—"

"Fuck 'em," Anders said. "I'm not scared of some pack from the Dark Ages. What, they're gonna chase us down in wheelchairs and club us with walkers?"

"I'll try to talk to Malachi," Hollis offered.

"Until then, be alert." Finn's voice was hard. "The Others aren't going to like this. Tomorrow, the world will know about Oscar. And I don't know what they'll do." Jessa would need a security guard, just in case.

"You know damn well they'll be out for blood," Anders said. "It ain't gonna be pretty."

"I still think now's not the time to reunite," Hollis said.

Because when they were together, the Others knew it. Somehow the five of them were linked. And that link grew stronger, more traceable, when they were close to one another.

"Maybe you're right," Finn agreed.

"Now's the time." Dante snorted. "Been a hell of a long time since I got to tear into some deserving son-of-a-bitch."

Anders laughed. "Can't wait to meet the pup."

"I'm sorry," Finn's voice was thick.

The line fell silent.

"See you soon," Dante said.

"Yep," Anders sounded off.

"Be careful," Hollis added.

And the line went dead. Finn sat there with his eyes closed, feeling exhausted, long after they were done. When he checked the clock next it was after midnight. He stood, stretching, and glanced out the window at the illuminated San Antonio skyline. The moon was covered with thin gray clouds, casting long shadows across the mish-mash of concrete and glass, parking lots and highways. He checked his phone. Both his head of security and his publicist had kept up a steady stream of emails and texts. Word of Cara's death was now public, as well as the possible birth of a child. He'd decided the best course of action was to make a statement before anyone else could beat him to the punch. He hoped, by making it public, he might offer Oscar some sort of protection.

In the ten years since they'd become infected, Finn and his pack had learned little about their adversaries. The Others. Hell, they hadn't known other werewolves existed until the Others pack jumped Mal. After that, they'd done everything they could to learn about them, with little luck. One thing they knew, the Others viewed Finn as a threat. But something seemed to keep them at bay. He'd seen them, knew they followed him from time to time, almost as if they were studying him. Not so for Mal. Three of them had come at Mal. If Finn hadn't been there… Well, Mal had barely survived the attack. Finn didn't think they knew about Anders, Hollis, or Dante. At least, they'd never been targeted or threatened. But with the Others, so much was unknown—including their motivation.

Bottom line, he needed to be prepared for the backlash that might follow.

The polite thing to do was call his parents and give them some advance notice. The phone went straight to voicemail.

"Mom, Dad, you have a grandson. He's home with me now. Just wanted you to know, since it'll be all over tomorrow's papers." He hung up, slid his phone into his pocket, and headed out of his office.

He was starving.

But the blended scents of Jessa and Oscar greeted him halfway to the kitchen. And finding Jessa in a tight gray T-shirt and plaid boxer shorts stirred a completely different sort of hunger. The entire day, the image of her pink bra and, the soft skin of her chest, had taunted him. He'd wanted to touch her. It had been hell not to.

And now? Jessa out of her business attire was even more beguiling that the well put-together young woman he'd come to expect. Her long blond hair fell to the middle of her back, curling softly. Soft, supple skin. Long legs, toned and lean. Willowy arms that cradled Oscar close while she swayed in time to the big-band music playing softly over the radio.

The wolf was riveted, focusing entirely on Jessa and Oscar. Proudly. Possessively. Finn felt it, too. And her scent, the swell of her breasts through her thin shirt, the curve of her ass, the purple polish on her bare toes... He'd never been so driven to claim a woman. It was primal, territorial. It had to be the wolf, not him. Or was it?

Oscar's soft whimper distracted him.

"Your snack is almost ready, Oscar," she said, speaking softly.

Her voice, soothing, entreating, made him calm. While he hoped his response to Jessa was based on her caring for his son, it was no less alarming. He didn't just want to take her to bed, he wanted to be with her. Better to take a long cold shower and put some space, and sanity, between them. Instead, he strode into the kitchen.

"A snack sounds good to me, too."

"Mr. Dean." She jumped. "I thought you'd gone out."

"Where would I go?" He glanced at her, curious to hear her answer.

She shrugged. "Wherever single people go?"

He grinned. "You're single, aren't you, Miss Talbot? Surely you have some ideas." But he couldn't imagine her frequenting the clubs he did. Or trawling for one-night hook-ups at a bar, for that matter.

She shook her head. "I don't have time to date, Mr. Dean." Which was a huge relief. He frowned, wishing he had a better rein on his emotions. "I was here. Working," he said, opening the refrigerator. "What did Augustina make this evening?"

"Oh, coq au vin. It was incredible," she said. "She's an amazing cook."

He put the plate in the microwave and turned it on. "But not much of a conversationalist." He glanced at Jessa.

She wrinkled her nose. "Not exactly."

He laughed. "That's okay. I don't pay her for the conversation." The microwave beeped.

Oscar squeaked then.

Finn glanced at her before carrying his plate to the table.

She prepared a bottle, shaking it, while still bouncing Oscar, on her way to the table. She sat, crossing her leg and propping Oscar on her lap. "Thomas has the crib set up but I've put Oscar in the portable bed in my room for the first few nights. Just so he doesn't feel alone—I hope that's okay?" She waited for his nod before continuing. She smiled at Oscar then said, "We received an email confirmation from the nanny agency. They'll begin working on a list of candidates and send files over in the next few weeks. So, I'll be able to start the weeding process quickly and be out of your hair."

His relief vanished, quickly replaced by something close to panic. Would she find someone who smiled at Oscar the way she did? Or hum to him? Or cradle him close, as if he were precious, not unwanted or…damaged? "You're very good at…that," he said between bites.

"You met one of the reasons why today," she replied. "Shelby, my sister, and Harry, Landon, and Nate. Each of them gave me a sort of hands-on internship." She had the most beautiful smile, the most brilliant eyes.

"What made you want to work for Dean?" he asked.

Her eyes widened. "Well, it's a noble company, doing good in a world that needs it." She paused. "But, honestly, there was definitely a financial component. Your company has a progressive advancement track, excellent insurance, some tuition perks, regular bonuses… All things a woman like me needs to take care of four siblings. They're smart, involved, but there's no guarantee they'll get scholarships or financial aid."

"So you gave up your dreams to take care of your family?" he asked, curious.

"I'd like to think I can do both. I blame you for that." She said, burping Oscar with ease.

"Me?" he asked, finishing his dinner and sitting back in his chair.

She nodded, shifting Oscar and getting him settled with his bottle before answering him. "I went to a seminar you gave at my campus. It was all about dreaming big and letting nothing stand in your way. Listening to you, I knew my dreams would never give my siblings *their* dreams. I'm their sister, but in a lot of ways I'm also their mother. Seeing them succeed is important."

"Do they know?" he asked.

"Know what?" she asked, her large green eyes finding his.

"Do they know you gave everything up for them?"

She frowned. "I didn't. Working for Dean Industries isn't a sacrifice. I feel lucky to be working for your company. And, no, I'm not just saying that because you *are* Mr. Dean. Is this where I thought I'd be now? No. But I didn't give everything up. And I wouldn't want them to think I had." She paused, smiling down at Oscar. "Besides, you—Oscar, needs me."

She'd been right the first time. "Where did you see yourself at this point in your life?" he asked.

She shook her head. "I don't really know. And it doesn't matter. I'm learning so much, and, I hope, I'm doing a good job where I am."

"I've heard as much," he agreed.

Her brows went up at the same time Oscar finished his bottle. She set it on the table and shifted him to her shoulder. Finn watched every move. She was so careful, so gentle, he could almost feel the tenderness in her touch. He wanted to feel it.

Oscar burped, making her smile.

"It's a little ridiculous how rewarding that sound is," she said, still smiling, her green gaze locked with his.

He didn't have much to say to that. Here he was, sitting in his kitchen, well past midnight, enjoying a conversation. It had been a long time since he'd spent time with a woman outside of a bed. As a matter of fact, he couldn't remember the last time he'd enjoyed a woman's company when some sort of foreplay wasn't involved.

He imagined her hair spread across her pillows and her cheeks flushed with pleasure. Would she feel as soft as she looked? Would she smile and sigh beneath him? Or would she be passionate and vocal? The wolf wanted to know— every instinct demanded he find out. He focused entirely on her, quieting his mind until he was in tune with her.

The flushing of her cheeks.

The pump of her heart accelerating.

The slight shudder of her breath.

The nervous dart of her tongue along her lower lip.

She swallowed.

Did she feel *this*?

She blinked, severing the connection between them.

"He'll be down for a few hours now, so I suppose I'll try to get some sleep." She stood. "Is there anything else you need me to do this evening, Mr. Dean?"

He swallowed back the laundry list of inappropriate things that sprang to mind. "No, Miss Talbot. Thank you," he ground out the last words. But there was something. "And you can call me Finn."

She paused, hesitant. "Good night, Finn."

His hand clenched around his fork, bending the metal into a knot. He cleared his throat. "Sweet dreams, Jessa."

She carried Oscar from the room, her scent lingering in the air long after her bedroom door closed behind her.

· · ·

Jessa glanced at the five dossiers she'd compiled, waiting for Mr. Dean's approval. She wasn't 100 percent pleased with any of the candidates, but she supposed there never would be someone truly up for caring for Oscar. In the two weeks she'd spent with him, she'd accepted the fact that he was the sweetest-tempered baby in existence. He fussed only when he was hungry, tired, or needed changing. Because of that, she'd been able to sleep well and accomplish the few tasks that needed to be done. Her brothers had stopped by to visit a few times, probably to keep her from discovering the state of the house, and they'd had homework video chats when needed. Since Finn had expressed concern over taking Oscar too far from him, she'd rarely left his apartment. She wasn't used to having so much free time, but Augustina refused to let her help with household chores.

Oscar was too little to put in a jogging stroller, but she'd taken him for a couple of brisk walks in the morning for a change of scenery. Finn insisted she have a bodyguard, but Greg, the man assigned to her, kept his distance, and after a while, she would forget he was there. Instead, she enjoyed the new city paths and parks, things Oscar would enjoy when he was older. On mornings that were too cold to venture out, she'd do yoga when Mr. Dean left for work.

Mr. Dean. Finn. She'd spent far too much of her free time thinking about her mesmerizing employer.

Worse, he'd taken over her dreams, consuming her with

his hands and mouth in a way that made her weak. There was something predatory about him. Something that made her stomach clench and her long-neglected body beg for attention.

In her twenty-eight years, her experience with men was limited. But never, ever, had she felt so…conscious of a man. As soon as he walked through the door, she was hyperaware of him.

To him, she was a temporary installation, nothing more. After that first night, he'd remained reserved and distant. He came home late and disappeared into his office, reappearing long enough to eat and exchange pleasantries.

Because I'm an employee.

Finnegan Dean would never think of her as anything beyond that. She needed to be careful. Falling for her boss would be a stupid mistake—one she couldn't afford to make, on so many levels. If her dreams weren't so real, she'd remember that. But they were, waking her up in a tangle of sheets and sweat, alone and aching, still with the whisper of his fingers on her skin.

She glanced at the clock. "I'm late," she murmured. But she couldn't exactly show up for a meeting covered in spit-up and smelling like sour formula. She shrugged out of the shirt and hurried into the bathroom, rinsing the formula from the fabric. She worked quickly, running the stain under water and lathering it with soap. She rinsed the soap and hung it over the shower rail before heading into her room. Only to find Finn staring into the crib at his sleeping son.

"Oh, Mr. Dean." She crossed her arms over her bra.

He looked up, his eyes widening. "You were late—"

"I was covered in spit-up," she returned, frozen in place.

His gaze swept up the curve of her arm, her shoulder, her neck, making her skin warm. She wasn't prepared for the way his jaw clenched. Or the "My apologies," he mumbled. When his gaze burned into hers, there was no air in her lungs. He stared at her, his hand gripping the railing of the crib, until she wasn't sure she'd stay upright. "I'll wait in my office," his growl was all the more startling, echoing down the hall as he left the room.

She slumped into the wall, sucking in air, staring at the open door. What was that? Was he angry? His time was precious, but surely he'd understand why she was late.

But standing there worrying over his reaction would only make her later.

She closed the door and changed quickly, slipping into a pink blouse and tucking it into the waist of her gray slacks. With a quick glance at a sleeping Oscar, she picked up the dossiers and the baby monitor and headed to his office. Analyzing his reaction was a bad idea. So was thinking about the way his gaze heated the skin of her neck and shoulder. To get worked up over a simple look was stupid. But it had been a long time since she'd been on the receiving end of such obvious masculine appreciation. He *saw* her—and possibly liked it.

Or, more likely, she was seeing what she wanted to see. *As if, Jessa.* Someone like Finnegan Dean would never be interested in her.

She shook off her thoughts as she knocked on his office door.

"Come in," he called.

She crossed the room and sat in the chair opposite his desk, immediately jumping into business. "These are the five candidates I've determined best meet the criteria you provided."

"I apologize for intruding, Jessa." He paused. "I'll knock from now on. It's your room."

She nodded, avoiding his gaze. Sweeping the incident aside was the best idea. She could pretend he hadn't caught her in her plain white bra. Not that wearing something more feminine or sexy would have made it better. She swallowed, sliding the packets across his desk. "Here are the files. I thought you might review them and give me your thoughts. That way I can begin interviewing next Friday."

"Next Friday?" He seemed surprised.

"You gave me a deadline," she reminded him. "I meet my deadlines."

He sat back in his chair, ran a hand over his face, and sighed. "It will wait until after we get back."

She let out her breath, slowly. "Get back?"

"I need to make a trip, four or five days. You and Oscar are coming with me." He glanced at her, then back at the files she'd placed on his desk. "I know it's short notice, but it's necessary."

She processed this. "I need to check in on Nate first. He struggles with his math work. Can Oscar and I—"

"Yes, go," his answer was short.

It would do her a world of good. Being so wrapped up in Oscar and Finnegan Dean was likely playing a part in her nocturnal fantasies. She needed fresh air, familiar faces, and adult conversation that wasn't centered around Oscar—as precious as he was. At the moment, the only things she had to do were care for Oscar and hunt for the perfect nanny. Which brought her back to the matter at hand. "Would you prefer to review these later?" she asked.

"I've cleared my schedule for the day, specifically for this purpose. Can you summarize their strengths and weaknesses?"

She nodded, having anticipated as much. "My pleasure."

"And the trip?" he asked. "Will it interfere with any plans?"

As long as it wasn't too far away. Her brothers seemed to be doing fine without her, but she still worried over them—something that irritated her brothers, especially Harry. She sighed. *Maybe a trip is a good idea.* "No. A trip might be nice."

His smile was breathtaking.

She sat, stunned. It was like she'd made his day, when it was the other way around. Her heart was thumping like mad, the strangest, warmest pull flooding her insides.

"So, the candidates," she said, clearing her throat.

He came around his desk and sat in the chair beside her, leaning close to read over her shoulder as she pointed out those things that had caught her attention. She tried not to get distracted by the tantalizing scent of his spicy aftershave or the way his shirt hugged the well-muscled contours of his upper arm. There was too much riding on this position. She could not afford to let him get to her.

She worked her way through the first three candidates before Oscar's high-pitched cry sounded through the baby monitor. She smiled, checking her watch, and stood. "Would you mind giving me fifteen minutes? I'll get him situated and return?" She offered him the dossier they were reviewing.

"I'll read over these until you get back." He glanced at the monitor.

She nodded and headed into her room. Oscar was in a full fit of temper, his little face red and his fists tight and flailing.

"What's the matter, Oscar? Are you starving, little man?" She cooed, picking him up and patting him. "Let's get you cleaned up and then we'll find you something to ease that ache in your little tummy, okay? I was with your daddy. He's worrying over you, wanting to find the best possible nanny."

Oscar had calmed a little, but started wailing when she changed his diaper.

"I know, sweetie, I'm sorry," she continued. "As soon as you have a dry diaper, everything will be better. I promise, okay? Be patient." She disposed of the dirty diaper and scooped him. "Now, let's go."

She worked quietly in the kitchen, humming away. When

Oscar had his bottle, she headed back to Mr. Dean's office. But instead of finding him pouring over the dossiers she'd made, she found him on the phone.

"You're sure?" He ran a hand through his thick black hair, his barely suppressed anger visible. "I can protect them."

She hesitated, a twinge of anxiety nagging the base of her spine. Finn's posture was ramrod stiff, his voice hard and edged with something almost…menacing. Maybe now wasn't the time to invade his office.

"I know this is bad," he muttered. "We'll leave as soon as I can. It's safer there."

Oscar chose that moment to burp, drawing Mr. Dean's attention. His expression shifted, from anger to concern. But his posture seemed to stiffen further, so rigid he seemed braced for something. Something scared Finnegan Dean? Her anxiety doubled.

He hung up, sliding his phone back into his pocket.

"I can come back," she offered.

"No," he said. "I should have let that go to voicemail." He shook his head, returning to his seat and flipping through the dossier with quick, tight motions.

"Is everything all right?" she asked, shifting Oscar from one arm to the other.

He glanced at her, defensive. "Nothing I can't handle."

She nodded.

"He likes the sound of your voice," he said.

"What?" she asked, startled.

"I heard you on the monitor. He responds to you."

She shook her head, far too pleased by his words. "He's too little to know. But hearing me lets him know he's not alone."

"Maybe." He held up the fourth dossier. "What about Mrs. Flores?"

She sat at his side, ready to work. He needed to make this

decision so she could get back to her regular life. A life that was full of practicalities and moved too quickly to indulge in fantasies about her boss. And, to safeguard her heart. She was getting far too attached to Oscar.

They spent another hour in discussion, narrowing the field to three candidates. And through it all, she kept Oscar in the crook of her arm. When she looked down, she saw him staring around, alert and awake.

"Well, hello, Oscar," she said, holding him close. "How are you?" she cooed. "Did you want to see your daddy?"

She didn't hold the baby out. Finn still wasn't ready for that—he'd made that clear. But she hoped he might take some interest in his infant son. Finding Oscar a nanny was a kind of interest, yes, but it wasn't the same thing as bonding with the boy, or falling in love with his watchful gaze and gurgling noises.

She smiled at Oscar. "Do you approve of our choices?" she asked, glancing at Mr. Dean.

He was watching Oscar, and he looked—wary. "Is he doing well?"

She nodded. "He's a champ. I admit my experience is limited to my siblings, but I'd say Oscar is one of the easiest babies ever."

Mr. Dean stood, moving behind his desk to sit. "That's good. Hopefully he won't drive away as many nannies as his uncle and I did."

She grinned. "Were you wild children?"

He nodded, arching a brow. "That's putting it mildly."

She sighed, knowing there was no reason for her to linger. "Is there anything else I can do for you, Mr. Dean?"

He looked at her, his smile melting her from the inside out. "I thought we'd progressed to Finn, Jessa."

She stood, cradling Oscar. Why did saying his name sound so intimate? "Finn." She paused. "Is there anything else?"

He sat back in his chair. "What do you think of the new tagline?"

His abrupt change of topic made her pause. Tagline? For the new sport hybrids? It had to be. That was the focus of the marketing department right now—chasing down the elusive demographic of drivers wanting fast cars that wouldn't leave a big carbon footprint. Not an easy task. "You mean: Dean Automotive, redefining smart and sexy?" she asked. "I happen to think it's quite good." And her idea.

"Because it's a good tagline? Or because it's yours?" he asked, steepling his fingers in front of him.

She hesitated, knowing this was an opportunity to remind him that her skill set extended beyond the domestic domain. "I take credit for it. Proudly. It's exactly the tone we want to set for this new line. Isn't it? Perhaps I am biased… But the test group seemed to respond favorably as well."

"I know, I've seen the numbers," he agreed, those unfathomable eyes riveted upon her.

She smiled.

"It's good work," he said.

"Thank you, sir." If she kept smiling like this, she was going to burst. "I'll let you get back to work."

He nodded, his gaze fixed on his computer screen as she pulled the door shut behind her.

A good day, overall. Yes, Harry was going to blow a gasket when she told him she was leaving town. Each day his phone calls were becoming more frequent, and longer. He was managing, but only just. And she understood. He had a life, exams, and responsibilities of his own. The house, their brothers, had always been her responsibility.

And yet, even he'd been blown away by Finn's generous offer. She didn't keep their financial situation from them—they all knew every cent counted. They'd promised to step up, to make this work, and come out ahead for a change.

Besides she couldn't leave Oscar—or Finn. Whatever was happening, Finn's tension was palpable.

I can protect them. Finn's words.

She shivered, holding Oscar closer and sitting in the new rocking chair. Who needed protecting? And from what?

Oscar lay on her lap, his little eyes red-rimmed and his mouth stretching wide in a yawn. She smiled, leaning forward to press a kiss to his head, and smoothed the copper curl on the top of his head. "Your daddy loves you, Oscar, he just doesn't know how to show it yet." She paused, stroking the baby's soft cheek. "We need to show him you're not something to be afraid of. You're something to love."

She sang her brother's favorite lullaby, rocking Oscar gently until he was sound asleep. Only then did the anxiety return. As irrational as it was, she couldn't shake the feeling that Finn's phone call had something to do with Oscar.

Chapter Four

Finn's fingers paused over his keyboard at the sound of Jessa's voice. She'd left the baby monitor on his desk.

It was no wonder that Oscar responded to her. When she wasn't talking to him, she was humming. If his son found comfort in her, he understood. In the last few days, he'd spent a surprising amount of time working from home. He'd tried to convince himself it was so he could be available if Jessa needed anything, but the truth was more complicated.

The wolf needed to be close to Oscar.

And Jessa, too.

Jessa.

He'd find a nanny, and then what? His wolf rejected—violently—the idea of letting her go. Finn's heart tightened and his pulse quickened, as if he were bracing for a fight. Against himself? Because the wolf wanted her?

He had no fucking choice.

How the hell could he function with Jessa as his assistant? Working closely every day, tempted by her scent, her voice, her eyes… What the hell had he been thinking? Even taking pains to avoid her, he still sought out the rhythm of her heartbeat. It was enough, however slight the connection. To lose that... He rolled his head, breathing deep to soothe the wolf.

But the wolf would not be soothed. Finn felt the heat in his blood. He, the wolf, couldn't let her go.

Even though keeping her only ensured he was putting her in danger...

He ran a hand over his face.

Anders had called. The Others were on the move. Whether they were coming his way or not, he needed to be ready.

He sent some of his security team ahead to the refuge. No point moving Jessa and Oscar there if it wasn't secure. Brown, his security lead, checked the apartment perimeter alarm and headed out.

The Others and Cyrus, their alpha, had been toying with them for years. The bastard had made his presence known not long after Mal's attack. Mal's recovery confirmed that he and Finn were wolves—no human could have survived. Since then, Cyrus could be tied to every accident that had occurred. A loose fuel line on his private airplane. An assistant being mugged and another receiving a faulty prescription that led to an almost fatal poisoning. A fire in his office building. The repeated deaths of his mother's prized show dogs. Occasionally, packets of pictures would show up—of him, the women he'd slept with, his parents, and Mal. No note, no prints, nothing traceable. But there was no denying the threat. If only Finn could understand why.

Why keep their distance from Finn? Why all the games?

Hollis theorized they were too scared to see what might happen if they killed Finn. Finn was alpha of their pack. Hollis believed their packs were genetically linked, so it was possible that Finn's death might damage both bloodlines. Now more than ever, Finn hoped Hollis was right.

A dull ache pulsed in his temples. It would be good to

return to the refuge, to turn off the noise that filled his mind and connect with his wolf. Too often, he ignored the need to run, to hunt, to indulge the animal inside his skin. If he wasn't careful, the wolf would force its way out and Finn would lose control.

The financial report on his desk held no interest. For the time being, he'd put the best interests of the company in the hands of his Chief of Operations and Chief Executive Officer. He had to.

As far as he could tell, his press release had no impact on sales. Apparently, taking in his orphan baby son didn't make him any less or more appealing to the consumer public, a fact he was incredibly thankful for.

Of course, Cara was being dragged through the mud. Anyone she'd ever been involved with was being tapped for potential scandal. Once or twice it had been hinted that he wasn't Oscar's biological father, something that would make his life ten times easier. And Oscar's as well.

He worked steadily, answering IMs and directing incoming information as needed.

His phone rang and he answered. "Mom?"

"Finnegan, we were out of cell range or we would have called sooner. What's this about a grandson?"

"Yes, Mom, a boy." He glanced out the window behind his desk.

"My, Finn. Well isn't that…nice? Will we get to meet him when he's with you? What sort of custody arrangement have you worked out?"

"He's mine. Here. All the time," he answered.

"But…but where's the mother? And who is she? Did your father and I ever meet her?" She paused. "She's not one of your party girls, is she?"

"Cara Bennett. She was a model. She died in childbirth." He spoke without inflection, choosing his words carefully.

"How horribly tragic. But what are *you* going to do with

a baby?"

"I'm going to raise him, Mom. With the help of a nanny," he added.

"Well, good luck with that, dear boy. We never had the best luck with domestic help," she said. "Your father says hello. We'll be back in a few weeks and will check in with you then."

"Fine," he said, his frustrating mounting.

"Good-bye, darling," she said before the line went dead.

He stared at his phone.

Oscar's cry made him jump. He hadn't turned off the baby monitor, enjoying the tenuous connection with his son. But now, with the high-pitched wail of his newborn son echoing off the walls of his office, the wolf was on the defensive.

Finn wanted a drink. And, maybe, he'd check on Oscar.

"Hey, hey, Oscar." Jessa's voice came over the monitor. "Oh, yuck, Oscar. How can something so little make something so nasty?"

He smiled.

"I think I'd be crying, too," she kept on talking. "What a smell. Ooh."

He heard shuffling and suspected she was lifting Oscar up.

"I think this calls for a bath." Her voice sounded strange, muffled. "And maybe I need to ask Thomas to bring me a gas mask next time he makes a delivery."

Oscar's squealing increased.

"What? You don't like Thomas?" she asked. "He's a very nice man. He's asked me to dinner, you know. And, between you and me, I haven't been asked out in a long time."

Oscar's cry softened. Finn frowned. Thomas had asked her out. He should give the baby department manager more credit.

"See, that's better isn't it? All dry. Let's get you a bottle and then we'll get you a bath."

He stood and headed into the kitchen, knowing full well she and Oscar would be there.

She was humming, of course, her back to him, a long golden ponytail swinging between her shoulder blades.

"Evening, you two," he said.

"Evening Mr. Dea—Finn." She smiled. "Joining us for dinner?"

"What did Augustina leave us?"

"I'm not sure. Oscar and I were dealing with a toxic waste spill in the bedroom."

"That sounds...distressing," he offered. He opened the oven to find a casserole dish. "Looks like chicken of some sort. With rice."

"Sounds yummy," she said, heading to the table with Oscar and his bottle. "Would you rather eat in the dining room? Augustina told me that's what you prefer."

He set the casserole dish on the table. "I suppose I did eat in the dining room."

She nodded.

He shrugged, hoping that was enough of an explanation.

He saw her slight smile.

He pulled two plates down. "Hungry?" he asked, wanting their company.

"Oh," she shook her head, flustered. "I'll wait until he's done. He needs a bath. Then I can eat. But thank you."

He put the chicken back in the oven. "I'll wait."

She looked at him, surprised. "You don't have to."

She was right, he didn't. He didn't need to eat in the kitchen with his *assistant* and the baby. He owned the house. He was her employer. The last thing he should do was spend more time with her... If anything, he should put space between them. Before this...this...connection twisted into something risky for them both.

But her green gaze drew him in, warm and honest. This

was where he wanted to be.

Space. *Now*.

"I think I'll go for a run." The thought of stretching his legs and sweating it out was vastly appealing.

She nodded. "Enjoy your run."

Did she look disappointed? Did it matter? He left the room without another word. He was angry, at himself. First he'd brought this on his friends, then he'd infected his son, and now he was going to pull Jessa into the mess? Because his wolf's possessiveness for her was justification enough to drag her into his world? Hell, no.

Of course, he'd become attached to her. She was caring for his son—a young, beautiful intelligent woman he also happened to have a raging hunger for. But attachment was a no-no. Hell, he'd made the goddamn rules.

He changed into his running clothes and set off, following the path the city had recently put in. The cool evening, buzzing sounds of the city, and the brilliant light displays offered his senses a good distraction. He ran until he was dripping sweat and breathing hard. And then he pushed on until his lungs were aching and his legs were on fire. It felt good to push his body—even if the wolf begged to take over. He could shift at will. Next week, the moon was full and the wolf ruled. But tonight, Finn kept control.

Control. He snorted.

Beyond the whole is-he-a-werewolf thing, Finn had far more mundane concerns. He didn't know a damn thing about fatherhood or what it meant to be a good, involved father. The thought of having to care for something so helpless terrified him. What if his son didn't like him? Jessa said the baby was too little to know the difference but Finn wasn't so sure.

Which brought him back to Jessa. Could he trust Oscar's care to someone other than Jessa? Did he want to…

By the time he rode the elevator to the penthouse, he was

wiped out. He stalked down the dark hallway, pulling off his soaked shirt as he went. He needed a steaming hot shower and a scotch. After that, he'd think about eating.

He paused at Jessa's door. It was cracked, but the room was dark. He pushed in, slowly, glancing at her bed. Empty. Oscar lay on his back in his crib. He crept forward, staring at the small bundle. Oscar was breathing rapidly. Too rapidly. He frowned, reaching out his hand in the dark, his palm against Oscar's chest.

His son. It was only Oscar's small, warm, body, the rapid thrum of the baby's heartbeat under his palm. And yet, Finn grew disoriented, short of breath, his skin scorched—as if his flesh had been branded. He stiffened, his hand, his palm, burning. Finn pulled back, clenching his hand and shaking his head. A million indistinguishable whispers filled his mind, a thousand unrestrained emotions clutched in on his heart. He couldn't think, couldn't sift through the noise or sensations. He stumbled out into the hall on unsteady legs.

"Finn?" It was Jessa. "Are you all right?"

His hand fisted at his side, burning, throbbing. "I… I'm good." He leaned against the wall, dragging in deep lung-fuls of air and focusing on Jessa's face. Her concern.

"Can I get you anything?" she asked.

Could she make the noise end? Make the heat singeing his hand stop radiating up the length of his arm and into his chest? He didn't know what was happening to him. Whatever it was, she couldn't help him. Why did she have to look like she cared—about him? And why the hell did being so close to her draw such a fierce reaction. "Where were you?" he snapped.

She frowned. "I was eating—"

"You left the monitor in my office." He stared at her, directing all his pent-up frustrations at her. "How would you have heard him if he needed you?" Maybe, if he was hard enough on her, she'd stay away from him. Maybe, if he pushed her away, he could stay away. "Something could have happened—"

She held up the monitor, her hand shaking. "I realized where it was after you went on your run. I wouldn't have left him otherwise." She hesitated then reached for him, her hand settling on his arm. "Are you sure you're okay? You might be overheated. Let me get you some water."

Her touch was a balm against his scorched skin. He glanced at her hand, terrified by the effect she had on him. He ran a hand over his face. "I'm sorry, Jessa."

"It's okay. I–I can't imagine what you're feeling. But..." She hesitated, drawing his attention back to her. "I'm here, if you need me for anything."

He hadn't realized he was reaching for her. Hadn't realized how soft the skin of her shoulders would feel beneath his fingers. But he shuddered at the contact. His hunger was hard and fast, gripping him so tightly that breathing was difficult. It would be so easy to pull her close, to take what he wanted. And right now, there was nothing he wanted more.

"Drink some water, Finn," her voice wavered as she stepped back, severing the connection. "I–I put your plate in the microwave."

He stared at her closed door. The wolf told him to follow her, to touch her again, claim her. So, he turned and headed toward the kitchen. No more thinking or analyzing tonight. No more revelations. He ate his meal and downed a gallon of water.

· · ·

Jessa navigated the stroller through the bustling farmer's market along the river, Greg the bodyguard trailing behind. She loved walking through the newly restored brewery and warehouse area. It was a bright autumn day, the air was crisp, the sky blue, and she'd been in desperate need of some fresh air. She'd hidden in her room until Finn had left, then packed them up for a long walk. She'd barely slept, caught up in whatever Finn had stirred to life the night before. He seemed to have some sort of power over her. His simple touch sparking a desire that had yet to fade. It scared her, to feel so strongly for a man that held her future in his hands.

A man she needed to remember was off-limits.

She shoved her brooding aside, and wandered through the marketplace. She and Oscar had made the trek twice already, enjoying the mix of people and quiet. She turned into the newly created park, admiring the small statues and public art that had been incorporated along the pathway. Wind chimes, gnomes, faces on trees—she pushed the stroller around a sidewalk artist working in chalk to recreate a Monet painting.

Oscar slept, so she wandered on. The autumn sun filtered through the mix of trees and shrubs to cast long shadows over the winding path. She shivered, moving into the sunlight and picking up the pace. Maybe it was the filtered light or the sudden silence, but she didn't like being so isolated, even if it was in her head. No sound, no birdsong, no voices. She kept going, startling at the sudden snap of a twig. She glanced back over her shoulder, but saw no one. It was Greg, that's all. He'd be coming down the path any second. But that didn't stop her from sprinting until she came out on a wider path. She caught her breath, slowing her pace as she smiled at a dog-walker, nodded at an ancient couple shuffling along arm-in-arm, and dodged a group of runners. Oscar fussed, it was time for his bottle.

She wasn't the freak-out type, but something felt off—

"How old is he?" the deep voice startled her. So did the pale blue eyes of the massive man suddenly walking at her side.

Soft alarm bells made the hair on her arms and neck prick up. Where the hell had he come from? It's not like he didn't stand out. He did. So how had she missed him? And she couldn't shake the sense she'd seen him before. She had. Maybe he lived nearby? And this was his jogging route. No need to get paranoid. Besides, Greg would be there any second. "A few weeks," she managed.

"A few weeks? Wow, you look great," the man said, glancing at her hands. "Ringless. Doing the single mom thing?"

"No," she lied. She spied the playground and tried to relax. She glanced at the path, searching for some sign of Greg. No need to panic surrounded by a dozen mothers, nannies, and twice as many children. "His father is meeting me here."

Pale blond brows rose. "Is he? Some guys have all the luck." He smiled, but it didn't reach his eyes. No, the look was the opposite of friendly. Alarm turned to fear, though she tried not to let him see it. She stopped by a crowded bench, hoping he'd walk on.

She glanced inside the stroller. Oscar wasn't fussing. He'd curled into a ball, absolutely quiet and still.

"I hate to sound cliché here, but do we know each other? Maybe a club? Or the gym? I feel like I…know you." He had an accent. Eastern European? Nordic? She wasn't sure.

"No," she said, worrying over Oscar. And there was still no sign of Greg.

He stepped closer. "You sure? My instincts are normally spot-on."

"Probably walking here," she answered, eager to send him on his way. Was he sniffing her? She sat, fighting the urge to run. Running would be bad. He would follow. She glanced at her phone, pretending she was getting a call. Where was Greg? "Need to take this."

He stepped back, looking inside the stroller once more. "I'll see you next time." He tipped his head her way and walked slowly down the path.

He was leaving. So why was it still so hard to breathe? Her heart was hammering, her panic relentless—even as he wandered farther away. She wanted to run but was too frightened to move.

Her phone rang, startling her so much she almost dropped it.

"Yes?" she answered, her voice odd and high.

"Where are you?" Finn snapped.

"Finn. Thank God. I mean, hey." She glanced down the path again, embarrassed when the woman on the bench beside her shot her a look.

"Jessa?"

"In the city park," she said, watching the pale blond man saunter slowly down the path. "By the old brewery."

"Something's wrong, I can hear it in your voice." Finn pushed.

"It's nothing," she clarified. "I think." She was overreacting.

There was a pause. "What's nothing?"

She glanced down the path, but the tall blond stranger was gone. Oscar began to wail. She scooped him up, holding him close to her. He quieted instantly. "It's probably nothing—"

"Then tell me."

"A man," she murmured into the phone. "He was just—a little too curious, too friendly."

"Where's Greg?"

"I don't know. He disappeared. It's just…I'm scared. This sounds stupid. Forget it, okay?"

"No. I'm sending Brown to you. Stay there."

"Who's Brown?" she asked.

"Head of my security team."

"Finn, I don't think that's necessary." She was mortified. What if the man *had* just been hitting on her? It could happen. But…she knew it was something more. She'd never been so afraid.

"I do." He paused. "What did he look like?"

"He was big. Tall. White-blond hair. Pale blue eyes." She shivered.

"I'll be there in five minutes. Do not move."

"Finn—"

But the line was dead.

She made Oscar a bottle and fed him, his solid weight a comfort. But her nerves were on edge. She knew it was ridiculous, that no one cared what she was doing, but she couldn't shake the feeling that someone was watching her. No matter how adorable the tiny dog wearing a sweater was, or how funny the kids were on the playground, she couldn't relax.

"That guy's back," said the woman on the bench next to her. Jessa glanced at her. "The big one you were talking to? He's at the end of the path on his phone."

"He is?" Her throat felt pinched. She shifted Oscar to her shoulder and patted him on the back.

Maybe he was a reporter? It made sense. Oscar was probably big news by now. But Finn's reaction was a little extreme for a reporter—surely.

"No offense if he's a friend of yours, but that guy is totally creeping me out."

"So it's not just me?" she asked, relieved. Oscar burped.

"No." The woman sat her book down. "He's watching you. Do we need to call for help?"

She shook her head. One quick glance told her the man was watching, his pale blue eyes hard and cold. He grinned, as if he knew she was aware of him. Pacing back and forth, he made no attempt to hide what he was doing. He seemed to enjoy the affect he was having on her. "Someone's coming to meet me," Jessa told the woman. "But thanks."

"Think I'll stay until they're here," she offered.

"Thank you," Jessa murmured, on the verge of tears. Finn would be here. Soon. But then she remembered his telephone conversation, and what he'd said. *I can protect them.*

"Miss Talbot?"

Jessa winced, shielding Oscar with both her arms, hating how terrified she was. This man, though, however big and burly he was, didn't have the same stalking factor.

"I'm Mr. Brown. Mr. Dean sent me."

Her relief was instantaneous. "Mr. Brown, the man is at the end of the path." She wanted to point, but she didn't.

Mr. Brown didn't turn his head. "I see him. And he sees me. It's important that we get you out of the park before Mr. Dean gets here."

"Should I carry Oscar?" she asked, standing quickly and slipping her purse onto her shoulder. "Did you find Greg?"

"He's safer in the stroller," he answered. "And I'm sure Greg is fine. Let's go."

She nodded, reluctantly buckling Oscar into his stroller. She smiled her thanks at the woman and hooked her arm through Brown's. "I told him I was waiting for the baby's father," she explained quickly. Though honestly, she needed someone to hold on to.

Mr. Brown nodded.

Her hands were shaking, so he took over pushing the stroller. "You're doing well," he said. "Almost to the car."

By the time Oscar was safely clipped into the car, Jessa was gasping for breath. She adjusted Oscar's car-seat straps, then held on to his little foot. She wanted Oscar in her arms, back in Finn's house. He yawned, his mouth forming a perfect 'O' before he drifted back to sleep.

She burst into tears, the panic she'd barely managed to hold at bay crashing into her. Was she losing her mind? No. The other woman felt the threat, too. But why had the man singled her out? Why wasn't the car moving yet? When the passenger door opened, she bit off a cry.

"Jessa?" Finn's voice was anguished.

She shook her head, covering her face with her hands. "He's fine."

"You're not." He climbed into the car and pulled her close, cradling her against his side. "But you will be. You're safe."

She nodded, turning into him—needing his strength. She hadn't realized just how terrified she was until now. Finn's arm was firm around her, his hand gripping her upper arm tightly. He felt good. Her nose pressed against the collar of his shirt, filling her nostrils with his heady scent. Maybe after a few hours of this, she'd be able to stop shaking.

His finger tilted her head back. "Look at me."

She did, mesmerized by the anger that blazed in his eyes.

His voice was low, "You are safe."

She nodded. "I feel like an idiot," her words shook. "He was just a man. And we were in a public place."

"Trust your instincts, Jessa." His fingers smoothed the hair from her face. "What did they tell you?"

"That he was dangerous," she answered. "That running would be bad."

"Why?" he asked, his eyes narrowing.

"It will sound crazy."

"It won't," he assured her.

She swallowed, whispering, "He would chase us." She watched his jaw clench. "Which sounds crazy. It does. *Nothing* happened. So why am I reacting this way?"

"You did the right thing." He took her hands in his, rubbing them together. "You're probably suffering from mild shock."

"From what? Some random guy being too friendly?" her voice rose. "I don't understand what happened?"

"He would have chased you. He would have chased Oscar." He waited, still rubbing her hands.

His words were hardly comforting. "What?" she asked, a

broken squeak of sound.

He shook his head, his hold tightened around hers. "Do you trust me, Jessa?"

She stared at him, still reeling from his words. "Yes."

He cradled her cheek in his hand. "Then trust me to take care of this." His phone began to ring. But when she would have moved to her side of the seat, he tucked her against him.

"Yes?" he answered. "He was here."

She tried to hear what the other person was saying, but no luck. The rough gravel of Finn's voice and the heavy beat of his heart drowned out everything else

"I want security at her home…" He paused, listening. "No. Now." Another pause. "No, I don't want him to know where we've gone. We need a distraction, something to throw them off their scent." He paused. "Get back to me."

He hung up.

"Finn," she murmured, still clutching his jacket lapel. His words were a blur. *Security at her home.* "Are my brothers at risk?" she looked up at him.

"No." His eyes swept over her face, his arm tightening about her. "But they'll have protection anyway."

"You have to tell me what's going on."

He shook his head. "You wouldn't believe me if I did." His smile was hard. "All you need to know is that man and I have a history. A violent history."

She shuddered. "But—"

"I think it's best if we leave a little early for our trip. Until this is sorted out." She heard the finality in his voice and pushed off his chest.

"Until what's sorted out?" She stared at him. "Thirty minutes ago I thought I was having some sort of mental break…thought I was imagining being followed. Now you're telling me I was right. And that because of your past with this man, my family needs protection—"

"They don't need protection," he argued. "It's a precaution."

"A precaution?" Her voice rose. "If that's supposed to comfort me, it doesn't. I'm not leaving my family."

"I'll move them, Jessa. Someplace they'll have around the clock security, drivers, and complete safety."

He meant it, she could tell. But to go to such extremes. "Why?" she pushed.

"Because I will do whatever it takes to keep you here, for Oscar. Your brothers aren't at risk. Oscar is." He glanced at the sleeping baby.

She shook her head. "You expect me to go without asking questions?"

"That's exactly what I expect, Jessa." His jaw was clenched, his desperation real.

"This isn't about my employment anymore. I need my brothers more than I need a job." She swallowed. "They are all I have in the world. Nothing can happen to them—"

"Nothing will." His tone was hard. "Nothing. You said you trust me." But then his gaze lowered, staring at her mouth. His nostrils flared ever so slightly, his lips parted. "Trust me. Please." The way he was looking at her made it impossible to argue. She did trust him, even now, when there were things she didn't know. He said her brothers weren't a target, but Oscar was. If they were trying to get to Finn or Oscar, surely those close to Finn were at risk. Not the nanny's family.

He waited, prepared to argue with her. But that wasn't what made her pause. It was Oscar, the soft gurgle he made in his sleep. Whatever want Finn stirred within her, she loved this baby. And, if her brothers were protected, how could she turn her back on Oscar? The answer was easy. She couldn't.

Chapter Five

Finn bit back a groan. He couldn't resist sliding his hand beneath her hair to cup her head, to stroke the soft skin along the back of her neck.

He'd never been as scared as he was today. Never been so ready to kill. Her voice on the phone had the wolf raring to hunt. But he needed to get to her, to Oscar, first. Even the wolf understood that. Seeing the car, hearing Brown's reassurances, hadn't eased him. Only pulling her close, capturing Oscar's foot in his hand, had chased his panic away. And once she'd been pressed against him, he'd been unable to let go.

Her breasts crushed against his chest, her fingers gripped his shirt front, the curve of her hip fit in his hand. All of him, man and wolf, wanted this woman. It was powerful—too powerful. The thick silver chain around his neck felt hot against his chest, reminding him to keep his head. The need to hold her, to touch her, to taste her was overwhelming. Her full lips parted. He could lean in, claim her mouth.

His wolf demanded it. As far as the wolf was concerned, she was his.

But he fought his wolf, the silver medallion singeing his skin. Losing control with Jessa would be bad.

The car came to a stop, jarring them both.

She was out of the car before he could say a word, unclicking Oscar's car seat and hurrying toward the elevator. He followed, the thrum of possessiveness still coursing through his veins. The elevator ride was silent, but he couldn't keep his eyes off her.

What made it worse was knowing she wanted him. He could see the thrum of her pulse in her throat. Smell her arousal in her scent. His hands fisted as he failed to shut her out. Her green eyes, when she dared look at him, begged for his touch.

Brown stood between them, looking stoically ahead.

While he stared at her, she focused solely on Oscar.

Oscar.

The reason Jessa was here.

He drew in a deep breath, reminding himself of the truth. She was not his. He had no right to her. This was her job. He would not give in to this attraction—it would only do harm.

By the time they exited the elevator, he'd regained some sliver of self-control. "Brown," he said, leading the man to his office.

"Mr. Dean." Jessa's voice stopped him.

He stared at her, wanting to buy as much time as possible. He was in control, for now, but he didn't know what to do, not yet. When it came to Jessa Talbot, he and his wolf did not see eye-to-eye. But she had a right to have her questions answered. Some of her questions. "I'll be there in a minute," he told Brown, following Jessa and Oscar into her room.

She was agitated, that much was clear, but he didn't know what to do about it. She said she trusted him. Now he needed her to do what he said. Watching her lift Oscar, press a kiss to his head, and place him gently in the crib, warmed his heart.

She lingered, running a fingertip along Oscar's cheek, before she turned those bright green eyes on him.

"My brothers and sister are all I have in the world, Mr. Dean," she said. "If I'm to stay with you and Oscar, I need your word they will be safe."

If I'm to stay... He swallowed, leaning against the doorframe. If she left... The wolf reared up in protest. Could he let her leave? Maybe he and the wolf did have something in common. He tried not to think about that too much.

He nodded. "They have my protection."

"From?" she asked.

He ran a hand across his face, choosing his words carefully. "The man in the park."

She wrapped her arms around herself, prompting him to reach for her. His hands covered hers, his thumbs stroking her satin skin. He didn't like the fear in her eyes, or the way she wavered on her feet.

"Why is this happening?" she asked.

He released her, pacing the length of her room. He was still too caught up in these new feelings to respond right away. His wolf wanted her to know...everything. Hell, his wolf wanted her as his mate. He froze, letting that realization wash over him.

He looked at her, at how frightened she was. This was what he'd done to her. By bringing her into his world, he'd introduced her to fear. And as much as he craved her, he knew it was wrong—for Jessa. She was human, clueless to the bullshit that was his world. Telling her would change that, erase it forever. He searched her face. Maybe he should let her go.

"I need five minutes," he said.

She nodded.

He had Brown dispatch bodyguards to the Talbot house, then he called Harry to explain the situation. Rather, that the paparazzi were getting a little determined and he thought some extra security was necessary. Harry sounded excited. Having a housekeeper, cook, and driver would make things easier, even if they would each have their own bodyguard for the time being.

But news that Greg was found, his neck broken, in a dumpster a few miles from the park had him raging. Cyrus had been with Jessa, so he hadn't been the one to kill the guard—meaning Cyrus hadn't been alone.

After splashing some cold water on his face, he returned to Jessa.

She was sitting in her rocking chair, eyes closed. If she didn't have a death grip on the chair handles, he might think she was sleeping.

He sat on the footstool and looked at her. "Once you know this, it will change everything."

She opened her eyes. "Everything's already changed, hasn't it?"

"Guess so." He shook his head.

She frowned. "Tell me why this is happening."

He rested his elbows on his knees. "When I graduated from college, I took some time to find myself. I drank and partied and made bad choices. But one good thing I did was help my brother on a dig in Montana. He was an archeology buff. Loved it." He stood, pacing in front of the windows. "I found a bone, not all that surprising on a dig but exciting nonetheless. It was old, very old. My brother was excited because he couldn't tell what it was—whether it was human or something else. He wanted it to be something else, something that would get him in a textbook or journal." He ran a hand over the back of his neck. "A dust storm blew in and we ran for cover, but the terrain was uneven and none of us could see. I fell on the bone." He lifted his shirt, showing her the puncture scar along his side.

She frowned.

"When I woke up, I was sick. My brother and the rest of the team were worried. But we were high up, the storm was going on, and no help was coming anytime soon. I remember passing out—" He broke off. "And I remember waking up…"

She stood. "What happened Finn?"

He looked at her. "My brother and his fiancée were dead. Mauled by an animal. A wolf. My friends had been attacked, too, though they were alive."

She frowned. "I'm so sorry, Finn. That's horrible. I had no idea."

"No one did. We couldn't tell the truth. People would lock us up and throw away the fucking key. A wolf attack? There had never, ever, been an attack like this." He agreed. "That bone was infected—made me infected. And, so far, there's no cure."

"Infected with what?" Her brow dipped. "But surely—"

"No cure. I've learned to control it, for the most part." He pulled the medallion from his shirt, holding it tight. "But it's there, a part of me, something I have to fight against every day."

"What do you mean, control it?" she asked, her expression wary as she eyed the medallion.

"The world thinks my brother and his fiancée died in a car accident. But I did it." He watched her. "I was the wolf that attacked, Jessa. Me." He waited, watching the disbelief on her face. "I was the one that killed my brother and his fiancée. That infected the only friends I've ever had. Me." He waited.

She shook her head. "I don't understand."

"You do," he argued. "But you don't want to."

"You're serious? You mean… Like werewolves?" Her voice was high-pitched, unsteady. "Finn, you can't believe this… Werewolves don't exist. It's impossible."

"I wish you were right." He glanced at her. "He's one,

too."

Her eyes widened. "The man in the park?"

He nodded.

She sat down, then, staring blindly around the room.

"You *knew* something was wrong. You felt it, didn't you?" he asked.

She nodded. "But this?"

"Cyrus wants to track down me and those I turned. To kill us, keep us caged, I'm not sure. But the birth of my son seems to have Cyrus and his pack on alert."

Her green eyes fixed on him, but she stayed silent.

"This is all about control. They, the Others, want ultimate control." He paused. "Jessa?"

"What happened to Oscar's mother?"

"She died in a car accident," he said.

"Did she?" she asked. "Like your brother and his fiancée?" It was a whisper but her point was made.

He opened his mouth, then closed it. "Hollis isn't sure what happened to her. She was found in a wrecked car." He waited, hoping she wouldn't ask about Greg. It was too much.

"What you're telling me—this is real?"

He reached for her hands. But she recoiled, tucking her hands under her thighs and leaning back into the cushion. He stiffened, nodding once. "It is."

She nodded. "This is a lot to take in, Mr. Dean."

The "Mr. Dean" was a kick to the gut. "And harder to believe?"

She didn't say anything—she didn't have to. The confusion on her face, processing everything he said, was plain to see.

"Cyrus wants Oscar?" She paused. He felt her panic, her fear. "Will Oscar change?"

"We don't know. None of us were born this way," he admitted.

"How will you know?" she asked.

"The full moon is next week. Anything is possible."

"So, that's real? Next week?" She brushed past him to the crib, peering down at Oscar. She stared at his son with such love it tore at his heart. "Oh, little one."

"I know." The words stuck in his throat. "Brown's concerned that Cyrus will think you are my mate. You told him you were waiting on Oscar's father?"

"I wanted him to leave," she said, her tone defensive. "If anything, he'll think I was with Brown—considering how hard I was holding on to him."

"Your scent," he started, breaking off. He had to tell her, if only to keep her close. "Your scent is mingled with mine. And Oscar's."

Her features tightened. "He smelled me," she whispered. "I thought I'd imagined it."

Then he knows you're mine.

He shook his head and stood, unable to take the distance between them any longer. "The wolf's sense of smell is important. They can scent pack relations—enemies, allies, and mates." He moved to Oscar's crib, content to be close to them both. "You are my pack. He'll know that now."

"What if I don't want to be part of your pack?" she asked.

Her words cut through him. "It doesn't matter what you want." His gaze held hers. "It has nothing to do with want. It's a fact."

"So you're saying I don't have a choice?" she asked, her eyes wide with horror.

"I won't make you stay, Jessa," he admitted, even if the wolf howled in protest. "But I'm asking you to. Oscar needs you. And so do I."

She tore her gaze from his. "I'd like to lie down while Oscar's still asleep."

"Just a minute. Come with me, I've something to show you," he said, going through the bathroom that adjoined Jessa and Oscar's rooms. He waited, pleased that she eventually followed him. "There should be no reason to use this, but it's here." He pushed open Oscar's closet, sliding his finger along the release of the hidden door inside.

The wall slid back, revealing a small safe room.

"Are you kidding me?" Jessa's voice wavered.

"You saw how the release works?" he asked. "The emergency release is here. There's a keypad in my office—it's the only other way to open the door. Other than from the inside, of course."

She stared inside.

"Jessa?" he repeated. "Did you see how the release works?"

She nodded.

"Hit this button and the door slams and locks," he said, pointing to a red button just inside the door. "It can only be opened from the inside, here," he pointed at the keypad. "The code is here." He showed her, watching her eyes get wider and wider. "Do you have any questions?"

She shook her head, backing out. She stared around Oscar's nursery almost blindly before heading through the bathroom to her room.

He followed, regretting everything. He shouldn't have told her. He should have made something up. But it was too late now. "Jessa…" How could he make her understand?

"This is a lot to take in." She stared past him.

That's the understatement of the year. "Are you okay?"

"I honestly don't know." She shook her head. "I don't know how to believe anything you're telling me."

"I know—"

"I don't think you do," her voice wavered. "This is normal for you. It's the furthest thing from normal for me."

Everything she said was right. He hated it—hated feeling helpless. "Is there anything I can do?"

"Please. Give me some time to myself." She wouldn't look

at him.

He left, closing her door behind him. He lingered, pacing, the need to watch over them pressing in on him. And when he heard Jessa's soft crying, the wolf was ready for a fight.

• • •

"A few more minutes," Jessa said, bouncing Oscar in the sling she wore, walking the length of the apartment again. The order she'd placed yesterday, before her disastrous walk, hadn't been delivered on time. Now her world was upside down and her nerves were shot. And while Oscar was a sweet-tempered baby, he couldn't go without formula. It was her fault—she'd been shaking so badly, so distracted, that she'd knocked the remaining formula onto the floor before she could make Oscar's bottle. Now Thomas wasn't responding to her texts or calls, so she'd used Klemps's emergency delivery hotline. She'd laughed at its existence once—now she just hoped the formula would arrive before Oscar's patience ran out.

She had to finish packing if they were going to leave in the morning. And she had to decide if she was going with them. Or if she'd be saying good-bye to Oscar and Finn. She'd talked to Harry and her brothers, who were excited over their fancy living arrangements. They thought it was to avoid paparazzi—if only that were true. The truth? Her eyes burned from a sleepless night and too many tears.

The doorman buzzed, "You have a delivery from Klemps', Miss Talbot."

"Thank you," she said, smiling at Oscar in the fabric sling she was wearing. "See, I wouldn't let you go hungry little man."

Oscar regarded her with his wide, light eyes.

"You're welcome," she murmured. It would be easier to choose if she didn't love Oscar. But she did, more than she'd ever imagined possible.

He gurgled, making her smile

She opened the door to find Thomas carrying a box of supplies. "Hi, stranger," she said.

"Hi Jessa." He coughed.

"You sick?" she asked, shifting Oscar's sling to her other side.

"I'm not sure," he answered, following her into the hall. "Something's going on."

Something was going on. Thomas looked terrible. His complexion was waxy and pale—almost grey. A light sheen of perspiration across his brow and upper lip, and his eyes… It was as if the color had faded out of them. He noticed her examination and scowled, stalking into the kitchen—moving so swiftly, Jessa jumped.

That was when she noticed Oscar. He'd gone silent and motionless, burrowing against her.

The stroke of warning along her spine was quick, but unmistakable. Even though she knew Thomas was no threat, that there was no reason to be so damn jumpy, she tightened the sling holding Oscar—freeing her hands but anchoring him against her.

"Jessa," Thomas called from the kitchen.

She followed, taking a deep breath. "Adjusting Oscar," she explained. "He's hungry."

"He's growing." Thomas said, stepping closer. "Looks like you're doing a great job with him."

"Thank you." She smiled, once more thrown by his appearance. "Want some water? An aspirin?"

"I'm fine." He shook his head. "You know, we need to plan our date." She saw the slight tremor of his hand as he rested it on the counter.

"We will," she said. The baby was too still, too quiet. Something was wrong. She swallowed, looking Thomas in the eye. The color. Just like Cyrus. Her chest felt heavy, compressed. "Did something happen to you?"

His smile was slow. She saw the hardening of his face, the pinched tightness about his eyes as he said, "Yeah, you could say that." He shrugged. "I got mugged last night. Jumped on my way home from work. Damn dog bit my leg."

The hairs on her arm stood straight up.

"A dog?" she repeated.

"I guess. Damn thing almost tore my leg off." He shrugged. "I've been feeling weird ever since."

"Did you go to the doctor?" she asked, moving to the other side of the island and pulling out a baby bottle. Three days ago, she'd be worried about rabies or infection. Not now.

Finn's words haunted her. *I infected the only friends I've ever had. Me.*

Had Thomas been infected?

She'd jolted awake last night, nightmares about Cyrus's near colorless eyes, and Oscar's reaction terrifying her. Now Oscar was just as still and quiet, like he was hiding. Because of Thomas.

Panic pressed in, clenching her chest and abdomen.

Thomas isn't Cyrus.

"I'll go," he said. "But I had this need to see you first. And Oscar. All I've been able to think about today is seeing you two." He followed her around the kitchen island, carrying a canister of formula with him. He placed it on the counter, but didn't let go. "You smell as sweet as a tulip, Jessa. You know that?"

She tried to smile as his colorless gaze bore into her own. She touched his arm, startled by the heat of his skin. "I'm worried about you. Can you go to the doctor this afternoon? I can make you an appointment."

He paused, a hint of sadness on his face. "No. I have to do something first." He shook his head. "Something that might be hard for you, Jessa." He cleared his throat, his tone shifting, thickening into an almost-growl. "I need Oscar, Jessa. He said he'd leave you alone if I gave him Oscar."

She couldn't freeze up. She couldn't fall apart. Oscar needed her. She swallowed. Her phone vibrated in her pocket, but she couldn't reach for it.

"You'll have to call them back later," Thomas said.

What the hell was she supposed to do?

"I don't understand," she said, hoping her panic wasn't obvious.

"I think you do," he argued. "I know about the park. He told me."

She shivered involuntarily. She had to think. Calm. Stay calm and focus. She couldn't run. There was no place to hide... Wait. The safe room. It was close. She could get Oscar inside—if she was careful. "He who?" she asked, stalling.

Thomas frowned. "Cyrus. He said hi, by the way. That he's not the bad guy here, Finn is."

Her stomach tightened. Finn was the bad guy? She remembered the anguish in his face when he'd confessed what he'd done to his brother. She couldn't imagine seeing remorse in Cyrus's pale gaze. Not that it mattered. She wasn't handing Oscar over to anyone. She needed time. She needed room to maneuver. "Oh?"

Thomas shook his head. "He stole their ancestor's bone, Jessa. Stole their mojo, you could say. And he won't give it back. And his pack? They're bad guys. More than a third of the missing persons in San Antonio? Finn's pack. And they're not missing, they're dead. He's a murderer. Your boss is a murderer. He killed his own family, for Christ's sake." He shook his head. "You're not safe here."

Thomas's mounting agitation made it hard to breathe. She wouldn't listen to him—she couldn't. Finn wasn't a murderer. He couldn't be. "You want to keep me safe?" she asked.

He nodded. "I care about you."

The sincerity in his voice tore at her heart. Whatever had

happened to him, he was still Thomas. Surely she could reason with him—after Oscar was safe. She stared at him. "You do? Give me a few minutes to pack him a bag?" She turned and headed down the hall, hoping he wouldn't follow—hoping he wouldn't pick up on her out-of-control pulse.

By the time she'd reached the nursery, she was vibrating with nervous energy. She picked up a bag, cradling Oscar close in the sling.

"I don't think he's going to need much," Thomas said behind her, making her jump.

She didn't want to think about what that meant. All she could focus on was getting Oscar to safety. Then she and Thomas could talk this out, could make sense of what was happening, and how they'd both been caught up in a world that shouldn't exist.

"I'll pack light." She smiled at him, heading for the closet. She pulled an item from the hanger, running her finger across the small emergency latch that released the panic room door. It slid silently open. She had to hurry. But before she could free Oscar, her head snapped back, her hair gripped tightly, a searing pain forcing tears from her eyes. Panic came crashing in.

"Jessa," Thomas's desperation washed over her. He tugged her hair. "I can't let you keep him. Give him to me."

The sling was too tangled. It took all her strength, all her focus, to ignore her fear and pain. There wasn't time to be scared. She gripped the closet doorframe and pushed off, shielding Oscar as they fell into the safe room, and kicking the red button with all her strength. Thomas lunged forward, the flash of fury on his normally friendly face terrifying her. The door slammed shut, the resounding thud of him bouncing off metal echoing in the small, concrete room.

"It's okay, Oscar," she whispered to the baby, gulping down air. Finn. She pulled her phone from her pocket, but there was no service in the room. He'd know, surely he'd know. He'd sensed it before when they were in trouble. The small space felt cramped, claustrophobic and isolated. And safe. Now she needed to come to terms with what happened.

This was Thomas. Thomas was her friend…

But one look at the monitors mounted on the wall told her otherwise. Thomas writhed on the floor—a twisted scream choked out. His body was contorting, twisting in a hideous way—shredding his clothes and his skin. She didn't want to watch, to see what was happening, but she couldn't look away. She stared, horrified and transfixed by what she saw. What was left wasn't human at all.

"Oh, Thomas," she whispered. But he was gone. In his place was a large wolf. A very angry, very aggressive, wolf. And he was charging the door. The metal shook, the impact echoing in the room. Over and over the animal charged the door, hell-bent on getting in. She crawled across the room, huddling in the corner and cradling Oscar close. Terror was a new experience, all-consuming and paralyzing.

"It's okay," she said, patting his little back. "We're safe." If she kept saying it, maybe she'd believe it.

But Thomas—the wolf—wasn't giving up. He paced back and forth before the door, scratching up the flooring, ripping the baseboards free and chewing through the drywall. The power of his attack left her shaking, pressed tightly into the corner. When he was done there, he destroyed the room. She watched, scanning the monitors for some sort of help.

But, if help came, they'd have to face Thomas. The wolf lifted his head up, and howled.

Oscar shuddered.

"Daddy's coming," she said. "All you have to do is wait. He'll be here." She knew it was true. Knew nothing would stop Finn.

Chapter Six

"Who's here?" Finn asked the doorman, not bothering to slow. His son was in danger. Adrenaline coursed through him.

"Just the delivery boy," the doorman answered.

He glanced back then. "Thomas?"

The doorman nodded, glancing from him to Brown. "No one else."

But Brown picked up on Finn's agitation, instantly alert. "What do you need?"

He yanked open the door to the stairwell. "In three minutes, cut the lights," he yelled as he raced up the stairs.

He closed his eyes, letting the fury of the wolf warm his body in preparation. Thought wasn't possible. Oscar. Jessa. The wolf took control, and Finn welcomed him. The shift was hard, driven by rage and pain. Every muscle stretched and tore. His shoulders snapped downward, his spine lengthening as he fell forward. His claws split through his palms to click against the concrete stairs. Raw instinct surged as fur bristled and his nostrils flared, pulling in scents—searching. The wolf was in charge now. Things like hesitation and restraint no longer applied.

Thomas's odor reached him, tainting the air with the rank mix of wolf, blood, fear, and anger. He burst through the door, an ear-splitting howl of pure frustration and anger greeting him.

Thomas was angry. A good sign.

His ears perked up. No Oscar. No Jessa. He skirted the kitchen, through the great room, and trotted down the hall.

Silence. Thomas had scented him.

He crouched, waiting. And then darkness fell. Brown had cut the power.

Finn waited. Thomas would come. Thomas, a new wolf with no control or awareness, too loud, too nervous, and too clumsy to realize how lethal he was. The new wolf stumbled into the hall, pausing, anxious. His nails clicked on the wood floor as he took a few steps and paused again. Finn let the wolf's fear build. Then he attacked. He was silent, his teeth clamping down on the new wolf's neck before he could react. Thomas's haunches gave out, his nails gouging the floor as he fought to get away. He spun and rolled, scraping fur from Finn's shoulder and neck, desperate to break Finn's grip.

But Finn held tight, hoping Thomas would give up.

The lights flickered back on, revealing a thatch of long, golden hair on the ground. Droplets of blood.

Jessa.

Fury rolled over him, choking him, pulling his wolf into the maelstrom of primal instinct. He growled, his jaws clamping tight. The spurt of blood was hot, metallic, and quick, filling his mouth, splatting onto the floor beneath them. In seconds, the new wolf—Thomas—hung limply from his mouth. But Finn's rage wasn't appeased.

Jessa's hair… Oscar.

He dropped the wolf and ran into Oscar's room, sniffing the mangled frame of the panic room door. He could smell

Oscar and Jessa, but he didn't know what he'd find inside. He forced the change, fighting the wolf back, ignoring the brutal burn and grind of bone and muscle aligning into his human form. He wouldn't heal as fast, but he wasn't ready for Jessa to meet the wolf.

If she was okay. And Oscar?

They had to be okay.

He didn't give himself time to adjust, but stood and leaned against the panic room door. Breathing was hard, his legs were unsteady, but his apprehension forced him to move. He had to get to his office, to the keypad. But the door slid open. The red haze that had clouded his senses slid away, and his wolf retreated. He could finally breathe, finally think.

Jessa sat in the far corner of the room, her knees drawn up, Oscar on her lap. Her green eyes fixed on him, haunted.

He closed his eyes, fighting nausea.

"Are you okay?" she asked, so softly he doubted she'd actually spoken.

He nodded, vaguely aware that he was bloody—and naked. "You? Oscar?"

"Yes," she murmured, her gaze unwavering. "Is he dead?" She was shaking, he could see that from here.

Would she hate him? He hadn't planned on killing Thomas. But her hair and blood… His wolf was pacing again, ready to defend her, to do anything it needed to protect her. He nodded.

"He was here for Oscar." Her voice was unsteady, thick. She pushed off the wall to stand, her arm supporting the sling with Oscar inside. "I tried to get Oscar inside, knew he needed to be safe. But I couldn't get the sling off."

Her words ripped through him. She would sacrifice herself for Oscar, and it gutted him. He crossed the small space, steadying her, his hands clasping her upper arms. "And you?"

"Thomas said he wouldn't hurt me." She was dazed, he could see that.

"He would have hurt you, Jessa. He would have done whatever it took to take my son." He knew what Cyrus was capable of. And thinking of Oscar or Jessa at Cyrus's mercy made his blood run cold.

"No, he wouldn't."

"Cyrus is his alpha. Thomas *must* obey him," he argued. "It's the way the wolf works."

She stared up at him, fear in her eyes. He didn't fight her when she shrugged out of his hold. "Oscar needs a bottle." But she paused in the doorway, taking in the devastation that had been Oscar's room.

"Jessa," his voice broke. "Go into your room and wait for me."

She spun, her eyes shining with unshed tears—and anger. "Don't order me around. Jesus, Finn, I need to… I'm just… Stop."

Finn ran a hand over his face and nodded. She was right. He'd had ten years to come to terms with his fucked-up reality. She'd had a day. And until now she hadn't known what, exactly, "his reality" meant. He watched her, aching to hold her, to touch her. "Thank you for protecting Oscar."

She nodded, her gaze lingering on his bare chest, then traveled lower. "I need…" Her whisper hitched. Her green eyes slammed into his, the ragged pull of her breath shaking him. "You're naked."

The shift from fear to need was a palpable thing. Her emotions were high. Her life had been threatened, her endorphins had taken over. She needed some sort of release. He swallowed, trying not to respond, trying not to think about all the ways he could help her find her release—over and over.

"Mr. Dean?" It was Brown.

"In here," he answered, glad for the interruption.

Jessa blinked, sucking in a long, deep breath. "Oscar needs a bottle." She walked around the shattered crib, torn carpet, and chunks of drywall littering the floor.

"Miss Talbot, I advise you to wait," Brown said.

Shit, Thomas. He'd shift now, from wolf to the man he was. That was the hardest part—and Jessa didn't need to see. He wrapped a shredded throw around his waist as he went.

Oscar's soft cries were building, a sign that his son was hungry—something Jessa would immediately respond to. "Brown, bring a bottle and formula to Miss Talbot's room," he instructed. "My son is hungry."

Brown, good man that he was, headed toward the kitchen.

Jessa was staring at him.

"I'm sorry, Jessa," he murmured.

"Can I leave?" she asked. "Would you let me go?"

No. You can't go. He couldn't let her. His hands fisted at his sides. "You're upset."

"Yes, I'm upset. Normal people would find this upsetting." She bounced Oscar absent-mindedly. "My worries consist of paying rent and tuition and electric bills, of being there for my family, of hoping I'll eventually find someone to love—that loves me." Her words ran together, her agitation increasing. "Being hunted or eaten?" She shook her head. "I'm not sure I'm strong enough for this. But…" She shook her head, sniffing.

"But?" he prompted.

Oscar's ear-splitting wail interrupted them.

Luckily Brown arrived with a bottle, and Jessa took Oscar into her room, closing the door behind her. Finn stared at it, calming himself until he could hear the steady heartbeat of his son, the soft humming of Jessa.

"Mr. Dean?" Brown began. "He's gone."

Finn pushed past Brown into the hallway. The floor was wet with blood, several paw prints trailing to the emergency

exit he'd broken through to get in. *Stupid fucking idiot.*
He'd been too worked up to make sure Thomas was dead.
"Get someone down there, Brown. He can't leave. Do you
understand me?" This was his fault.

Brown nodded. "Yes sir."

Finn ran down the stairs, the senses of the wolf sharpening
his ears and nose. The scent of blood was easy to follow,
ending at the third floor—the parking garage. The door was
ajar, a thin strip of blood along its surface. But the trail ended
sharply, gas and rubber signaling the way Thomas had gone.

"Someone was waiting," Brown said, still scanning the
concrete garage floors.

Finn felt the fury of the wolf, but fought it back. "Cyrus,"
he said, glancing at his security chief.

Brown had a vested interest in destroying Cyrus, too, one
that made him unfailingly loyal to Finn. Eight years ago, Cyrus
had killed Brown's wife and taken his daughter. It was Finn
that had found Brown, broken and furious, and listened to
the man's too-implausible-to-be-true story. Except it wasn't.
He'd vowed to help Brown find his daughter, and the man
had been loyal to Finn ever since.

"I'll find them," Brown said.

"No, send Gentry. I need you to help get Oscar and Jessa
to the refuge." His voice was hard, inflexible. He wanted
Cyrus dead—wanted to rip the bastard's fucking throat out.
But he'd have to wait. Brown's revenge would have to wait,
too.

Brown stared at the ground, the streak of bright red
blood, and nodded.

It was enough. Finn spun on his heel and ran back up the
stairs. All that mattered was Oscar and Jessa. Seeing them,
smelling them…hearing the thrum of the blood in their veins
and the beat of their hearts would calm him. And so would
getting them to safety.

• • •

Jessa stared down at Oscar, the lids of his blue eyes growing heavier as he finished off his warm bottle. His little body relaxed, the latch on the bottle easing, as he drifted off to sleep. She smiled, stroking her finger along the soft curve of his cheek.

She envied Oscar. He had no idea what was going on. As long as he had someone there to take care of him, he was content. He didn't know anything about danger or fear. Or have to worry about anything beyond baby-things. He'd grow up thinking it was normal for men to turn into animals, to act like animals—with instincts to hunt and kill.

She sniffed, the tears she'd held at bay overwhelming her. She lifted Oscar up, propped his tiny body against her shoulder, and patted. When he burped, she almost burst into tears. She loved this baby. So much. She'd no idea just how much until today. And while any rational person would be packing up and leaving, she couldn't do it.

"Jessa?" Finn's voice was soft, anguished.

She shook her head, refusing to look at him. That would only make things worse. He was the other reason she couldn't leave. The hold he had on her refused to budge. Until she figured out what to do about it, she'd cling to Oscar and try not to fall apart.

"Take the laundry, divide it up," Finn's voice was tight, clipped. "All of this stays."

"The scent trail needs to be covered," a voice Jessa didn't know.

She opened her eyes, regarding Finn and the redhead at his side.

"You think soiled diapers and dirty clothes will throw them off?" the man asked.

Finn rubbed a hand over his face. "What else can I fucking

do, Hollis?"

The man, Hollis, shook his head. "I don't think they'll come back right away."

"That's why we're leaving," Finn said, looking at her. "We have to go, Jessa."

"Let me take her," Hollis said.

She froze, glancing at Hollis then at Finn and the look on his face. Fury. "No." His one word said it all.

"Oscar?" Hollis was exasperated.

"No," he repeated.

"Now you're going all territorial?" Hollis shook his head. "Think, Finn."

Finn spoke clearly. "I'm not letting either one out of my sight."

Hollis nodded, stepping back. "Fine. Take them. I'll do what I can here and meet you later."

Finn clapped the man on the shoulder. "Thank you."

Hollis's grin was tight. "What choice do I have?"

Finn's jaw clenched, his hand sliding from Hollis's shoulder.

Jessa waited, watching Finn's shoulders droop when they were left alone. "Who was that?" she asked.

His blue eyes found her. "Hollis. One of my oldest friends."

Exhaustion weighed her down. "Where are we going?"

"Someplace safe," he said, crossing to her.

She stared up at him. "When are we leaving?"

A ghost of a smile crossed his face. "Now."

She stood, unsteady. "Okay."

In ten minutes, they were climbing into a car she'd never seen before. She buckled Oscar into the car seat and tried to breathe but the throb of her head reminded her that Thomas had left his mark upon her—physically and mentally. She reached back, probing the wound and wincing. The gash felt deep—her hair was sticky and matted. When he'd done it, she'd barely registered what was happening. The burn of tears made her close her eyes.

She shouldn't think about Thomas.

She shouldn't think about anything.

They changed cars several times. Finn was there at her side, his voice encouraging and his hand on the base of her spine. It helped keep her fear at bay, even as exhaustion crept in. Sometime before dawn, they checked into a hotel. She had no idea what city they were in, but the hotel was all glitz and glamour, with crystal chandeliers and perky desk attendants going on about room service and spa treatments. She let Finn do the talking and carried Oscar to their room. Baby supplies were waiting on one of the beds, but Oscar was still sleeping. She pressed a kiss against his forehead and took a shower, washing her hair and standing under the water until she was too tired to stay on her feet. She tugged on the robe hanging on the back of the bathroom door, changed and fed Oscar, and collapsed on the bed.

Finn made phone calls—lots of phone calls—and the even pitch of his voice gave her some sense of calm.

But when he finally turned off the light and headed for the shower, sleep wouldn't come. She was aware of the guests next door, laughing and talking loudly, and the faint ding of the elevator down the hall. She heard the water running in the shower then Finn getting into the other double bed. He tossed and turned, punched his pillow into submission, then flopped back onto the mattress. His sigh echoed in the room.

Every squeak Oscar made, every creak of the mattress spring, Jessa's eyes would pop open and her heart would pound.

She turned, rolling onto her side to stare at the sliver of light that spilled in at the edge of the window. She heard the creak of Finn's bed, heard him pad across the floor to the bathroom and come back minutes later. But then there was silence. She jumped when Finn's hand rested on her hip.

"You need sleep," he whispered.

She didn't argue or pull away from him. Her heart thundered, yearning for his touch.

The mattress gave as he climbed onto her bed. He didn't say a word as he wrapped himself around her. His arm, thick and heavy, slid around her waist. His heat seeped through the terry-cloth robe she wore. And it felt good. Too good.

She closed her eyes.

His hand rested on her rib cage. His breath fanned the skin at the nape of her neck. One muscled calf slipped between hers, his toes brushing the inside of her foot. She was more distracted than ever now. But in a completely different way. Her body hummed, alive and awake.

Chapter Seven

What the fuck?

His wolf was happy.

So, why wasn't he? Why was he lying here aching for more? She was in his hold, so damn close he could feel every breath, every beat, every shudder. He could smell her soap and shampoo, her skin, the faint tang of blood, the scent of her arousal…for him.

She wasn't asleep any more than he was. She'd been through hell today. From the slight tremor in her hands as she'd fed Oscar, he knew she was barely holding it together. He'd wanted to offer her comfort—instead he'd put them in a precarious position. The last thing she needed was him coming on to her. Still, he wanted her. She wanted him. He was hard and throbbing, needing her.

But acting on it had permanent consequences.

His wolf wanted her as his mate—an unbreakable bond. A bond that would ensure Jessa never had a normal life again.

He lay there, taking slow, deep breaths, willing his heart to slow down. She dropped into an uneasy sleep, her body going limp and pliable in his arms. His brain wouldn't shut off. He'd worried about Oscar, but she'd keep him safe. And that scared the shit out of him. The woman in his arms had no idea how important she'd become to him. He turned, pressing his nose along the curve of her jaw and the soft skin along her neck. She could have been killed. He could not lose her.

It was a long night. Nightmares kept her from a deep sleep. Every whimper or twitch had him whispering reassurances in her ear. He rolled onto his back and pulled her close, trying not to react to the feel of her hand on his bare abdomen, or the exquisite torture of her breath on his chest. He buried his nose in her hair and forced himself to relax. He'd be no good to either of them if he didn't get some sleep.

When he woke up, Jessa was changing Oscar on the other bed. She was speaking softly, her smile so sweet he ached.

Oscar's long leg kicked out, catching Finn's attention. A little hand popped up—his son stretching and wriggling. Finn sat up, watching with curiosity. *So, small. So, perfect.*

He stood, and smiled as the baby's eyes tried to focus on him.

Finn chuckled.

"Breakfast," Jessa said, offering him the bottle.

She was the most beautiful thing he'd ever seen. Her long blond hair fell over one shoulder. Her huge green eyes were shadowed but bright. She smiled at him, offering him the bottle.

Reaching out, he took it.

Her smile grew.

I'd do anything to see that smile again.

Whipped? Yep. And I don't care. That should have scared the hell out of him, too, but it didn't.

She pointed at the chair in the corner and then placed his son in his arms. At first, he wasn't sure what to expect. Then something inside of him shifted. Protectiveness, yes, but more gentle. A certainty and rightness that seemed to center him.

She grinned at him again, saying, "He's a champion eater."

After a large bottle and two burps, Finn had the pleasure of studying his son. He took the time to note each dimple, ten toes, ten fingers, light eyes—like his own—and a strong grip. As Oscar drifted into a happy sleep, Finn accepted that something fundamental had changed.

He—and his wolf—felt purpose. He had every reason in the world to keep going, right here in this room. He'd never choose this life, but it no longer made sense to fight who and what he was.

Not with the Others tracking them.

Hollis said they were still sniffing around the Hill Country. Dante and Anders agreed. For now, they had an advantage. One they'd need. They had a long way to go today.

He stood, carried Oscar to the bed, and pressed a kiss on his soft cheek. "Sleep on," he whispered, placing him on the bed. "I will protect you, no matter what."

Jessa was combing through her hair with her fingers. He saw her wince and moved to her, lifting her hair aside to see the gash Thomas had left. His anger, the wolf's anger, rose instantly. "Hurt?"

She shrugged. "Only when I touch it." She turned, looking up at him.

"Did you get any sleep?" he asked.

She nodded. "Thank you for…that."

"For what?" For doing what he wanted?

"For keeping me safe," she finished.

"You are safe." He drew in a deep breath. "What you did for Oscar, protecting him—"

"I had to," she said softly.

"You had to put yourself in harm's way to protect my son?" He shook his head. "You're an amazing woman, Jessa. I can never, ever, repay you or thank you enough for what you've done for me." His throat grew tight, it was all he could manage.

Her cheeks colored, the slight hitch of her breath intriguing him. "I know he's not mine, but I love Oscar as if he were." Her voice was a whisper. "You don't need a nanny. You have me. No matter how scared I am, leaving him would kill me."

"Don't leave. Stay with him. Stay with me." He tilted her chin back. "Please. I will keep you safe."

She swallowed, her green eyes holding his. "With you, nothing's safe."

"I would never hurt you, Jessa. You protected my son with your life, risked everything for him—for us." He ground the words out, the pain of her doubt all but crippling. "You know what I am. My wolf and I will make sure nothing like this ever happens again. You are family now. My family. Do you believe me?"

Her eyes widened, but then she leaned into his hand, her nod slight.

His resistance almost crumbled. He ached to tug her close and kiss her lips. His wolf paced, craving a bond with her. His thumb traced the edge of her lower lip before he could stop himself. It was a mistake, an-oh-so-sweet mistake.

He stepped away from her, his control on the brink. He didn't want to leave her, but staying here was too great a temptation for his wolf. He slipped into his jeans and stepped into his boots, tugging on his white undershirt as he opened the door. "Getting breakfast," he said before he left the room.

• • •

She pulled on the jersey dress and frowned. Mr. Brown had already thrown away their old clothes, including her bra. Every trace of their route had to be destroyed, wiped out, to keep the Others off their tracks. Jessa understood, but now she had no bra and an indecently tight dress to wear. There was nothing she could do about it. According to Mr. Brown, they were leaving in five minutes.

She braided her hair loosely, brushed her teeth, and hurried back into the hotel bedroom. Oscar was wriggling and content on the bed, in a clean diaper and thick gown—since it was colder where they were going.

She smiled down at him. "You look happy."

The door opened to reveal Finn and Mr. Brown, both of whom immediately noticed her lack of bra. *Great*. She picked up Oscar, using him as a shield of sorts. "We're ready."

"Good." Finn's eyes narrowed. "Let's go."

They took the back way out, stairwells and parking garages, none of them talking until they were inside a truck. Oscar's seat was strapped in the middle, so she buckled him in. A motorcycle was strapped into the back of the truck, something she hadn't expected. No room for a car seat there, she grinned. But then, Finn was known for liking fast things.

When he climbed into the truck, her stomach tightened. Should she bring up this morning? He'd wanted to kiss her, so why hadn't he? She wouldn't have resisted. She would have held on—tight. Because damn it all, she loved him.

Instead of saying anything, she just sat in silence.

"Breakfast," he said, offering her a brown paper bag.

She took it. "Thank you."

He didn't say much as they navigated out of the city and onto a stretch of endless highway. She didn't know if it was her imagination, but the tension between them seemed to grow with each passing mile.

She finally broke the silence. "Can I ask a question?"

"Yes." His blue eyes glanced her way.

"What about Thomas's family? Will he just disappear? Is that what happens?"

"Yes."

"I'm guessing there's more like Thomas? Because of Cyrus?" she asked.

He nodded.

"Why do they hate you?"

His hands tightened on the steering wheel. "The bone that infected me was important—something they want. Hollis says it was probably one of their ancestors, possibly the same bloodline, but ancient. Which makes me and those I've turned more powerful than they are."

"He wants you because you're a threat. You challenge his role?"

He nodded.

"I'm guessing the whole territorial wolf thing prevents sharing and playing nice?"

He laughed. "Yes."

She loved that sound. And that smile. It made her heart happy. *He* made her heart happy. She swallowed.

"He might not want to kill me, but there's no doubt he wants to control me. A wolf is unfailingly loyal to his offspring. And his mate." He glanced at her, his hands clenching the steering wheel again.

Did he miss Cara? Their relationship had brought Oscar into the world. "I'm sorry about Oscar's mother. Was she... a wolf?"

"No. She had no idea what I was." He shook his head.

Jessa saw the sadness on his face. "You miss her?"

"Cara wasn't my mate. Sex isn't the same thing. She and I had a good time, nothing more." He looked at her. "A wolf only has one mate in his or her life. And once they find it, there is no one else."

Which meant he only had one thing at stake. "You have to protect Oscar. How do we do that?" she asked.

He ran a hand through his hair. "Stop fighting my wolf."

She turned in her seat. "You fight your... wolf?"

"Sometimes more than others." His grin was hard.

"Over what?" she asked.

His brows rose. "Domination. I'm an alpha, a leader.

Sometimes the wolf needs to prove that."

She had a vague idea what that meant. His run-in with Thomas was etched into her memory. "But you said Cyrus doesn't want to kill you."

"If the blood that runs in my veins is linked to his ancestors, then killing me might kill him."

"Oh," she sat back, digesting this.

"It's Hollis's theory. One I've never had to test."

She looked at Oscar, sleeping peacefully in his seat. "My brothers?"

"Are safe," he answered immediately. "Under constant guard."

"By werewolves?" she asked.

"No. None of my pack has turned anyone, Jessa. We don't look at this as a good thing. My pack—there's five of us— check in occasionally, but we know being together for too long tends to stir *recognition*. I talk to Hollis more often, for obvious reasons. He's our science guy—my answer man. He thinks it's an infection he can cure. Until then, we agreed: no children, no mates, no complications."

She stared at him. "Are you serious? So you're all supposed to suffer alone?"

He looked at her. "Versus pretending to live normal lives? Risk hurting people we care about, or infecting them? Hell, yes."

"No one should be alone," she said. "You have Oscar now."

"We don't know how this will affect him, Jessa. He's so small—" He broke off then, clearing his throat and sucking in a deep breath. "The change, turning, might kill him."

"Finn." But words stuck in her throat. Oscar was at risk? Whatever fear she'd felt before couldn't compare to what she felt now. This time she couldn't save him. "When will we know?"

"Four nights," Finn growled. "Then I'll go looking for Cyrus."

His words ended her need for conversation. But now the darkening sky seemed more threatening than Cyrus. There was nothing either of them could do to stop the moon.

Chapter Eight

Finn tried not to tense as he pulled into the driveway. It wasn't that he was unhappy to see Dante and Anders. It had been a few years since they'd all been together, and a day didn't go by that he didn't feel their absence. But the circumstances of their reunion were far from ideal. All too soon they'd face a full moon. Damn, he was tired.

"Hollis was at your apartment. Who are the other two?" Jessa asked from beside him in the truck cab.

"The big one next to him is Anders. He thinks he's hilarious." Anders waved, grinning. Dante crossed his arms and leaned against the porch railing, watching them. "And the other is Dante."

"How do you know one another?" she asked.

"College," he said. "We were all pretty close. Before I attacked them." Not anymore. Now he had no idea what they thought about all of this.

The passenger door opened before he'd unbuckled his seat belt.

"You must be Jessa." Anders was all smiles. "Nice to meet

the girl who didn't run away screaming."

Finn saw Jessa's smile and calmed. "Does that happen a lot?" she asked, laughter in her voice.

Anders nodded. "Hell, yes. You start sprouting pointy ears and a bunch of extra teeth, and you'd be surprised at how fast a gal can run in heels."

Finn saw the shock on Jessa's face before she said, "Maybe you should save that for the second or third date?"

Anders chuckled. "I'll think about it."

"Got here just in time." Hollis was at his door.

Dante stayed where he was. "Snow's coming in."

He glanced at the white sky. "Estimates on how much?" he asked, sniffing the air. He didn't want them trapped here. But a few feet of ice and snow would slow down anyone who might be looking for them—and cover their scent and tracks.

Dante shrugged.

Finn climbed out of the truck, unbuckling the car seat and pulling it with him. He saw the question on Jessa's face and nodded slightly. No, he didn't normally carry Oscar. But now, he needed his son close to meet his family.

Hollis smiled. "He's growing."

"Looks small to me," Dante argued.

"Babies generally are," Jessa said.

Dante's eyes narrowed, his gaze sweeping over Jessa from head to toe. Finn's wolf went on alert.

She shivered, her gaze seeking his. "It's cold."

"No wonder. Where's your coat?" Anders asked.

Which reminded Finn what she was wearing—and her lack of bra. "Here." He shrugged out of his flannel shirt and draped it over her shoulders. It helped, but not enough. "Inside," he snapped, anxious to find her something to wrap up in. He stayed close by her side as they made their way into the massive wood cabin he considered his real home.

Jessa was rubbing her hands together by the time they

were inside.

He tried not to stare at the hard, tight evidence of just how cold she was. And his wolf was pissed as hell that the others were seeing it, too. "Fire's this way," he said, nodding into the great room.

"I should probably clean up Oscar first," she said. "And get his bottle ready."

The other three seemed to be circling, equally curious about Oscar and Jessa, and the energy had his alpha on high alert. He'd get Jessa and Oscar settled then deal with the other three.

"My room's this way," he said, carrying Oscar with him.

He could breathe easier once he'd closed the bedroom door behind them.

"Is everything okay?" she asked, her soothing touch a whisper across his forearm.

He looked at her, covering her hand with his. "Why?"

"You're tense. I thought being here would be better." Her green eyes searched his.

He loved the way her hand tightened on his, like holding on to him made her calmer, too. He shook his head. "It's been a long time since we've all been together." Well, almost all. Mal wasn't here. "Takes some time for us to adjust. The wolves need to settle down." He set the car seat on the bed.

"Go. Get adjusted." She smiled. "I'm pretty sure Oscar would like some wriggle time out of that seat."

"I'll go." He paused. "But I'd feel better if you stayed in here with me." He saw the way she looked around the room. "I can sleep on the floor."

She glanced at him, her cheeks coloring. "Do you want to sleep on the floor?"

He swallowed. "No."

"You don't have to sleep on the floor," she whispered, shivering slightly, her gaze locking with his.

Sleeping with her the night before had been equal parts heaven and hell. And tonight he'd endure it again if it put her back in his arms. "Cold?" He took her hands in his. Soft and ice-cold.

She shrugged.

He grinned. "Give me a sec." He dug through his clothes, pulling out some flannel pajamas, thermal underwear, and an old sweatshirt. "They'll be big, but warm." He liked the idea of her wearing his clothes.

She took the clothing. "Warm is good."

He nodded, making his way to the bedroom door. "You have what you need for Oscar?"

She nodded.

"I'll be back." He paused. "Stay here."

She frowned, then nodded, and he closed the door behind him.

They were waiting for him in the great room.

"She's the *nanny*?" Dante asked, clearly not buying it.

"She's his mate," Hollis interrupted.

His wolf agreed. But Finn wasn't ready to admit defeat. Jessa deserved better.

"She's hot." Anders grinned, flopping into one of the large leather armchairs and propping his booted feet on the coffee table. "Damn hot. My wolf likes her. A lot."

Finn shook his head, ignoring his wolf's irritation.

"Oscar's so damn little." Dante's concern was surprising. "The change could break him into a million pieces."

Finn didn't argue. Fear had a vise grip on his heart, shredding his insides to bits. He'd never dreaded a moon so much in his life.

"If we can do it, he should be able to," Hollis interrupted again. "Oscar is part of us."

"Poor kid," Anders joked.

"Not really. He was born this way. He has a distinct

advantage over us." Hollis smiled. "Speaking of disadvantages. *When* Jessa and Finn bond, she'll have almost as much sway over you as he does. Alpha. His mate."

"Great," Dante said.

"She's not going to be my mate," Finn snapped.

All three of them looked at him.

"You can't fight instinct, man." Anders shook his head. "If we can feel what's going on with you two this strong, I can only imagine what you're fighting."

Finn ignored the comment.

"So we're all supposed to pretend she's not one of us? She's up for grabs?" Dante asked. "Meaning she's fair game? Like Anders said, she's hot."

Finn glared at him, hands fisted, jaw clenched.

Dante and Anders exchanged a look, laughing.

"And Oscar?" Hollis asked. "He's bonded with her. He clearly looks to her as mother."

Finn nodded.

"She'll need protection," Dante sighed. "She needs to know what's coming."

"She has an idea," Finn said, sitting.

"What's the plan?" Anders asked.

"Keep them safe. Rest a few days, before the change. I...I need to stay with them," Finn said, staring into the fire. His wolf would do whatever was necessary to protect him, he knew that. There had been no sign of the Others, but he had to stay close, he knew that. "Can you run the perimeter?"

Anders and Dante nodded.

"The pack will help," Hollis offered.

Ever since they were infected, Hollis read everything he could find on wolf habits, packs, and hunting, as well as werewolf lore. So far, their pack shared more of the true wolf's sensibilities that those of the Hollywood werewolf. Something Finn was thankful for. The only distinguishing difference between his pack and the native timber wolves that populated the refuge was size and strength. His pack was bigger, with longer snouts, pointier ears, larger teeth and claws, and brutal strength. What he was capable of in wolf form was hard to accept. Out of fear or respect, the native wolves welcomed them into the pack when the moon ruled.

"I'm counting on that," Finn nodded.

"As a point of safety…" Hollis's tone drew Finn's attention. "You need to be focused, Finn. You're the alpha. If you're distracted, we're distracted."

"So, do the deed. Make her one of us." Anders grinned.

Finn rose, pacing before the fire. "I wouldn't have wished this on any of you. You expect me to ask her to be part of this clusterfuck?"

"Seems to me she already is," Dante said. "If you didn't want her involved, why the hell did you bring her here?"

"To protect her," Finn snapped.

"Back up." Dante sighed. "Why hire her in the first place?"

"I needed a nanny. She has life-experience—"

"No, at the company. Before Oscar," Dante pushed.

"I didn't. I don't hire every employee at Dean Industries. Believe me, I wouldn't have." But it was a lie, and he knew it. Her scent was all it had taken. If she'd come in for an interview with him, he would have known then. She was important, someone he needed to keep close—but not too close. Now he couldn't keep his distance. When she was near, he wanted to touch her, to hold her, to reassure himself that she was there, safe, at his side. His wolf and his heart had already claimed her.

"Right." Dante stood. "I'm going to bed."

But after they'd turned in, Finn sat drinking a scotch and staring into the roaring flames of the fire. His wolf put Jessa's safety in jeopardy. He ran a hand over his face, trying not to remember the feel of her body beneath his hands. He closed his eyes, drawing in the echo of her scent, the sigh she made in her sleep. Until he got a firm rein on his hunger, he'd stay where he was—away from her.

He played a game of pool against himself, threw darts for the better part of an hour, and stared out the window at the falling snow until his eyelids grew heavy. Only then did he knock back the last of his scotch and head to his bedroom.

Oscar was sound asleep in a portable crib. And Jessa slept in the rocker, twisted awkwardly, her long hair spilling over the chair arm to the floor. He hesitated, knowing he should leave her—not touch her—but unable to stop himself. When he lifted her in his arms, she turned into him, her breath warming the cotton of his white undershirt and making his medallion hot. It didn't matter. The damn thing could burn a circle on his chest and he'd still be yearning for the feel of her curves pressed against him. He lay her on the bed, staring down at her. His wolf was pacing, hoping, and craving. So Finn headed for a long cold shower and ignored the wolf's temper.

Chapter Nine

He felt Jessa wake on the bed next to him, her body stiffening at the sound of howling. Lots and lots of howling. There was no break—when one ended, another began. The sound filled the room, offering him security, and her fear.

"Easy." He spoke softly against her ear. "They're just getting ready for tomorrow."

She drew in a wavering breath, her body trembling. There'd been no howling the last three nights, and she'd slept easy in his arms while he'd lain awake, wanting her. She'd managed to make herself at home, even with the uneasiness amongst his pack. They all knew she was his mate and were tired of his foul mood and short temper as he refused to admit the same. The pack laughed it off, but Jessa was hurt by his indifference.

Until they went to bed. It was hard to stay indifferent when she was in his arms.

Sleeping with her made everything better—and so much worse. While she'd had sweet dreams, his wolf demanded what he couldn't take. Her reaction now, shivering from the howl of the wolves, proved his point. But she had every right to be afraid. After what she'd seen, what she'd learned, the world was no longer a safe place.

She pressed closer to him, stirring all the hunger he'd spent hours bottling up. He pressed his eyes shut, knowing what he should do.

Leave the room.

Put distance between them.

Reassure her she was safe—with words, not touch.

Instead, he rolled behind her, spooning against her back and draping an arm around her waist. The contact made his wolf sit up and take notice, but the chain around his neck grew hot—reminding him to be careful. "It's what wolves do," he said.

"Do you understand them?" she whispered, rigid in his hold.

"Sort of," his voice was gruff. "Their intent."

She shivered against him, still uneasy.

"It's okay, Jessa. You're safe." But was she? His hand pressed against her stomach, offering—and taking—comfort in the contact. His palm warmed, the energy between them alive. She relaxed, making it that much easier to mold himself around her. The slight increase of her pulse made him pause. He swallowed. When he spoke, his words were a whisper. "Touching you comforts me."

"Yes," she murmured, the feel of her hand on his arm instantly pulling him in. The need to claim her was overwhelming. All it took was that touch, light and soft... almost timid. What would it feel like to have her touch him with confidence? Ownership? He wanted that, so much. A strange noise, part growl, tore from his throat.

She lifted her hand. "I'm sorry."

He rolled onto his back, grasping for control. He was the one that should be sorry, not her. "Don't be," he ground out.

Her words were low, harsh and ragged. "I feel like your wolf. Like you're fighting...me. Something you don't want, but can't let go of." She slid to the edge of the bed.

She was right—he couldn't let go of her. He lay there, reining in the need to show her what she did to him. He gripped the silver medallion. How could she understand what she was to him? If he gave in, she'd never be free. Protecting her from himself was the right thing to do.

His wolf wanted her to know, to understand. To feel what she did to them and who she was.

Protecting her meant keeping her warm, not letting her shiver on the side of the damn bed. He slid to the bedside, sitting as close as possible without touching her. The words rose in his chest, the wolf demanded he speak. "Jessa—" He broke off, his lungs emptying. He looked at her. "You know what I'm capable of. What do you want from me?"

Her green eyes shone, raw with hunger—hunger his wolf wholeheartedly approved of. She didn't understand. She needed to understand.

"Do you remember what I said in the truck?" he asked.

She blinked, her lips parting.

"A wolf has one mate. One." And his wolf was waiting, ready. He swallowed, standing to pace before the fire. *Say it. You're mine.* The wolf would rather he showed her. But throwing her down on the bed and giving her what she thought she wanted didn't seem like the best idea.

"And...and sex isn't the same thing. I know." She kept talking, her voice wavering—uncertain. "But I don't understand what's happening between us," she added, her words thick and strained. "I've never been so...drawn to a person. If this isn't what you want, why is it...this way between us?"

He stared at her, the roar of blood in his veins and the drum of his heart making it hard to focus. Drawn to him? Isn't that what he wanted?

"You act like there's nothing between us, but there is. We're connected." Her cheeks flushed. "You want me close, so close I can feel you want me, but I can't have you." She stared at him. "What about what I want?"

She wanted him. But she didn't understand what that meant. What if she wanted to leave him? What the hell would he do then? She was his mate. If the bond was sealed, he couldn't let her go.

"Or is it the wolf that wants me, but not you?" She shook her head. "I don't understand any of this." She was angry. "Tell me. Explain it so I can understand." He heard her uncertainty—her frustration.

Like him.

And his control was slipping. The wolf was winning. For once, Finn wanted him to win. He wanted to claim her. "A connection?" he repeated, crossing the room in two long steps. He gripped the blanket wrapped around her and tugged her to her feet. "I wish it were that simple."

Her eyes widened as she whispered, "Finn—"

His voice was gruff and hard. "This isn't about sex, Jessa." His tilted her chin up, forcing her to look him in the eye. He hadn't meant to sound harsh, but dammit, he couldn't stand hearing the doubt in her voice. He never wanted to hear it again. She stared at him, stunned. "This is about you, choosing me. No going back. No leaving. My mate. You are mine. Always."

"You—"

"I won't tie you to me. To this life. I can't," he continued. "So, yes. I fight."

"Stop fighting," she whispered.

He froze, his mind reeling, his fingers twisting in the blanket he'd pinned her in. She didn't mean it. She couldn't. He shook his head, denying the urge to pull her against him, to bind her to him. The wolf circled, howling in frustration, forcing Finn to hear her—to accept it.

She stepped closer, her hand covering the medallion that rested on his bare chest. "I choose you." She shivered, her eyes locking with his.

"Do you understand what you're saying, Jessa?"

Her fingers traced along his jaw. "You're mine. And I am yours."

He clasped the back of her head, fighting the wolf's hunger even as he held her close. He ran his nose along her hairline, a strange thrum of heat and a prick of pain tightening his chest, stealing the air from his lungs. "Always, Jessa. The wolf—I—won't let you go. I can't."

Her green eyes burned. "Never let me go," her voice hitched.

He gave up, and the wolf took over. If this was what she wanted, he couldn't fight her. She'd given herself to him, and the need to possess her was undeniable.

The last threads of rational thought and restraint slipped away. His hold tightened, hard and desperate, cradling her head, pulling her against him as his lips captured hers. She shuddered, her fingers gripping his shoulders as his tongue delved between her lips. The heat of her mouth, the broken gasp of breath, the tentative stroke of her tongue against his, had him lowering her to the bed beneath him.

There would be time to love her, to explore every inch of her. But right now, the wolf needed to seal their bond. Finn needed it.

He pushed his boxers off and kicked them aside, his hands already slipping under her flannel nightshirt to pull the fabric up and over her head. She helped, tugging the sleeves free and tossing it over his shoulder. He stared down, enthralled by every curve. Her skin was smooth, the small birthmark under her right breast the only mark on her. She was breathing heavily, watching him—waiting. And the instinct to fill her erased all else.

His hands clasped her hips, sliding her to the edge of the bed. "I'm not sure I can keep control. I want you so bad."

She nodded, the erratic rhythm of her breathing inflaming him further. "Lose control. Love me now."

He stood, so hard he hurt, staring down at her. She was beautiful, soft and eager. Her hands gripped his forearms, her green eyes fixed on his face, waiting. He ignored the painful singe of the silver against his neck and chest, and lifted her hips. No one had ever looked at him like this, had accepted him as he was. He held her gaze. Even as he traced his thumb across her taut nub, as she arched up and against him, as the pulsing tip of his erection slid just inside the tight heat of her body, his gaze remained locked with hers.

He groaned, his hands tightening on her hips.

Her nails dug into his skin, her breath escaping on a tight hiss.

He slid deep, her body stretching to accommodate him.

"Finn." His name. His Jessa. His mate.

Something shifted inside him, chipping away at the wall around his heart, the isolation he'd used to stay strong. No more. His heart and that of his wolf's aligned, beating as one. A sharp pain sliced through is chest, his lungs convulsing so tightly he could not move or think or breathe. The scar at his side was on fire, throbbing. The wound felt new, agonizingly raw. He curled in on himself, grinding his teeth against the remembered tear of bone into flesh. For an instant, he froze, struggling to stay upright as his gaze bored into Jessa's.

She moaned, her hands tightening on his arms. "Finn?" It was a broken whisper.

He drove into her, the pain easing the more he moved. The more he moved, the more she responded. Her hands slid up his arms, running over his shoulders. Her nails raked his back and buttocks, pushing him on. Her head fell back, her eyes closing.

"Look at me, Jessa," he murmured. He heard the command in his voice, knew she heard it, too. Her green eyes fluttered open. It was more than this overwhelming drive to join her body. In her eyes, he saw the acceptance of their bond. That she wanted this. That she wanted him. He could feel the rapid beat of her pulse, her body constricting tightly around him. Her breathing was shallow, almost panting. He wasn't the only one drowning in this. And it felt right.

He bent, dropping a kiss against her lips, leaning into the touch of her hand on his cheek. He moved with a frenzy he didn't understand. He didn't want to hurt her, but there was no easing the wolf. Groaning, he cradled her face between his hands, and kissed her.

She stared up at him, the need in her gaze shameless.

His hand slipped between them, his thumb sliding over the tight nub. He stroked the smooth flesh, smiling at the high-pitched whimper she made. He watched her face, her parted lips, the slight crease between her brows. His lips latched onto her nipple, tongue and teeth working the hardened peak until her hands fisted in his hair. He didn't stop until he felt her climax, the rhythmic clamping of her body constricting around his rock-hard erection.

He arched into her, wanting more, to be deeper. To leave her, even a fraction of an inch, drove the wolf into a frenzy. He thrust deep, mindless, seeking, burning. His heart clenched, gripped in an unseen vice. His release slammed into him, forcing a cry from his lungs—from deep inside. He braced himself over her as wave after wave of pleasure and pain wracked his body.

She held on to him, her soft hands clinging to his sides, sliding to his hips. As the fog of release cleared, his heart pumped frantically.

Only then did he realize what he'd done. They were mated, his wolf was happy, but he'd lost total control. And, for the first time in his life, he'd had sex without a condom.

• • •

Jessa couldn't move. Her heart was pounding, her lungs were scrambling for air, and every cell was processing what had just happened. She hadn't known what to expect, if it would be different for her. Yes, she'd picked Finn as her partner, her mate, but she wasn't a wolf. She didn't know what, exactly, would happen. If anything. But different wasn't the right word. Never in her life had she experienced anything like that.

"Jessa?" Finn's voice was low, soft.

She opened her eyes. He was beautiful, braced over her, breathing hard. She hadn't expected to know, with absolute confidence, that he was hers. "Hi."

He grinned, dropping onto his elbows to kiss her. She welcomed the kiss, her hands sliding up his back to hold him close. But then she lifted her hands, remembering his reaction to her touch earlier.

"Touch me," he said against her lips.

She smiled.

He pulled back, his gaze searching hers.

"I thought it hurt you," she explained.

He shook his head. "Not now."

"But it did before?" she asked, running her hands up his back. Her eyes widened. "Because you were fighting me?"

He closed his eyes, arching into her touch. His gaze met hers. "No more."

She nodded. "No more."

He kissed her again, his mouth soft, teasing. His breath fanned across her cheek, stirring a response she'd been sure he'd exhausted. But she wanted him now even more. Until the pain started.

She gasped, clutching at her side.

"Jessa?"

She pushed at him, needing air, needing to curl tight and cover her side.

"What's wrong?" He was desperate, his hands smoothing the hair from her face.

"I don't know," she hissed, the agony blinding her to everything. She curled into herself, pressing her hands to her side, but she couldn't escape the pain. "Oh God, Finn." She buried her face in her pillow, terrified she'd scream. What was happening? And how the hell could she make it stop?

Finn's hands were on her, the sweet agony of his touch making her cry out again. He pulled her into his lap, pressing her close. "Jessa," his finger tipped her face back. "What is it? Please tell me." His seemed voice faint.

She couldn't think, couldn't speak. The tearing in her side was a pain she'd never experienced. Beyond the pain, there was recognition—as if memories she'd long forgotten suddenly reappeared. They were faint, hints of things that were completely foreign yet oddly familiar. And it scared her. Violence. Fear.

So much pain.

She was vaguely aware of moving. Of voices. Of crying out when someone touched her side. Finn touched her then, she knew it was him. His touch eased the pain instantly.

"I'm sorry, Jessa." She felt his hand on her forehead and turned toward his whispered words. "This is my fault."

How was it his fault?

None of this was his fault. When she could talk, she'd tell him.

But the darkness closed in on her, and Finn faded away.

She dreamed.

For so long, she was walking in the dark.

Wolves came, lots of them—following her. And she wasn't afraid. Until a large white wolf came. Cyrus. She ran and ran. Finn was there. Finn as a wolf. He was big, his brown coat dusted with snow as he circled her. His blue eyes were the same, watching her with such intensity she knew she was safe. But when she followed Finn through the woods, she lost him. Somehow, she ended up at her house. Thomas was having dinner with her brothers. Thomas, with long teeth and wild eyes. She pounded on the windows but they didn't hear her. Thomas did. Time seemed to slow, her brothers and sister moving in slow motion. She saw the look on his face, the way he smiled at her before he attacked her brothers. There was nothing she could do but scream.

"Jessa?" It was Finn's voice. "Please wake up." She heard the anguish in his voice but couldn't open her eyes.

Chapter Ten

It took a lot of effort to pry her eyes open. How she'd become so trapped in sleep, she wasn't sure, but she couldn't shake it off. Her eyes were all but glued shut, and her body felt weighed down by a ton of bricks—centered on her extremely sore side. The more awake she was, the more vivid the pain. She pressed a hand against her side, startled by the uneven skin.

She blinked, her eyes adjusting to the sunlight that spilled into the room.

Oscar?

She sat up quickly. "Shit," she hissed, pressing her hand to her side. She was naked. She pushed the sheets down, revealing a scar. What the hell had happened? She and Finn… She was flooded with warmth. He hadn't hurt her. So how had this happened?

She stood, favoring her side, and moved to the crib.

No Oscar. But here at the refuge, they were safe. Finn must have him. Knowing that eased her worry. She hobbled into the bathroom, turned on the lights, and stared at her reflection. The scar resembled a puncture wound, with fine thin, lines radiating out, like a starburst.

Exactly like Finn's.

She turned, seeing an almost identical scar on her back. Her fingers lightly traced along the hyper-sensitized flesh, marveling. He'd marked her, irrefutably. And she liked it. Even if it hurt like hell. She leaned against the counter, unsteady on her feet. She slowly brushed her teeth before turning on the shower.

The waterfall shower was heaven. She braced her hands on the wall, letting the hot water ease her stiff side. The more relaxed she was, the more memories surfaced. Finn. His eyes. The feel of him inside her. She ached, the craving so overwhelming she leaned against the wall.

Washing her hair was hard work. Her side ached miserably, so she did the best she could, resting now and again.

"Need help?" Finn's voice.

She glanced over her shoulder at him. "I think I've got it," she answered, smiling.

"You're weak." His hand rested on her belly as his chest pressed against her back. "I would have helped you."

"I'm fine," she assured him, the thrill of his touch on her skin electric. She shuddered, hissing at the pull on her side.

"You're hurting." His fingers traced the scar on her back. "I'm sorry."

She turned in his hold. "About?"

"Scarring you." His hands clasped her face.

She shook her head, smiling at him. "No one can doubt I'm yours now."

His jaw tightened before he eased her close. His forehead rested against hers. "You wouldn't wake up," he murmured. "You were hurting."

"I'm fine," she repeated.

He tilted her head back, searching her face with his clear

blue gaze. She swallowed, reeling from the possessiveness on his face. "I wasn't," he said. "I can't see you hurting. I can't." The last word was a growl.

She kissed him, standing on tiptoe to twine her arms around his neck. It didn't matter if it hurt her side; he needed comfort, and she needed to give it to him. "How long have I been asleep?" she asked.

"Eleven hours."

And just like that her scar—all her aches and pains—seemed unimportant.

Tonight was the full moon. "Where's Oscar?" she asked, the tightness in her throat pinching her voice.

Finn's gaze met hers. "He's with his uncles. He's in good hands."

But that didn't ease the flare of panic she felt. "Tonight?"

He nodded.

"What can I do?" she asked.

"Stay with him." He kissed her, his jaw tightening before he added. "I can't stop the change—"

"I know." She nodded. She'd be alone with a house full of wolves. And Oscar. "Is…is there anything I can do to help him? If he needs help?"

He shook his head. "If it happens, there's nothing any of us can do."

She closed her eyes, pressing her forehead to his. "I'm scared."

His arms tightened around her. "He'll be okay. He's my son."

She nodded, wanting to believe him.

"You need to eat," he said, reaching around her to turn off the shower. "And clothes."

She followed him from the shower, letting him dry her with a fluffy black towel. He knelt, gently stroking the scar on her back with his fingers. Then her stomach. He kissed the scar, resting his head on her stomach. "I didn't know."

"I know." She ran her fingers through his wet hair. "Would it have changed anything?"

He looked up at her, the hunger in his eyes instantly igniting her need. "Maybe…"

She frowned, staring down at him. "Finn—"

"I can't hurt you." The edge to his voice was sharp, insistent…and wonderful. He cared about her, deeply. She felt it. "You're beautiful," he whispered, his gaze feasting on her bare body.

She smiled. "So are you."

"I want you." The rasp in his voice made her quiver. "I need you." His hand pressed over the thatch of hair between her legs. His nose traced the inside of her thigh, his breath a caress on her skin. Her hands gripped his shoulders, holding herself up as she arched into his touch. But the pain in her side caught her by surprise, white-hot and searing. She froze, her hand clapping over the scar and muffling her whimper.

He was up, swinging her into his arms when she would have crumpled. "Jessa? Shit," he growled. "Dammit."

She wanted to tell him she was okay, but it hurt too much to form a coherent sentence. When he lay her on the bed, she grabbed his hand and pressed it against the scar.

"Wait," she whispered, his touch easing the pain.

He stared at her, concern creasing his forehead. "This helps?" he asked.

She nodded, letting his warmth seep into her. It did. If it were possible, she'd think his touch was healing her from the inside. Beneath his hand, she felt stronger, the pain reduced to a dull ache.

He sat on the edge of the bed, his palm all but glued to her side. The other stroked her wet hair from her face, his fingers tracing her temple and jaw. His eyes burned with something. Not hunger or passion but anger…and maybe, regret. She didn't like the way he seemed to withdraw from her, even with his hand on her body.

"Finn, stop," she said.

When he would have lifted his hand, she held it in place.

"Stop thinking whatever you're thinking," she said.

The corner of his mouth kicked up. "Now you know what I'm thinking?"

She shook her head. "Not exactly. But I don't want to see…regret on your face when you look at me."

He blew out a long breath. "I did this to you."

"I will heal," she argued.

He shook his head. "Nothing will ever be the same, Jessa."

"I know." She sat up slowly, letting go of his hand. "But I have you. And Oscar. So, everything is better."

He stared down at her, his expression unreadable. He turned, pulling some long john pants and one of his flannel shirts from a dresser, offering them to her.

She buried her face in them. "They smell like you."

He pressed a kiss to her temple. "Come on." The words were hoarse. "You need to eat. And Oscar misses you."

She let him help her get dressed. She was already feeling better, but there was no denying she was tender. When she was dressed and she'd run a comb through her hair, she turned to find Finn frowning at her.

"What?" she asked.

"You're too distracting."

She smiled. "It's a bad thing that you find me distracting?"

He gripped her shoulders in his hands. "I don't want anyone else to feel this way about you." His face hardened. "I don't think I'd handle it well."

She shook her head. "I'm yours."

He nodded. "Yes."

"Knowing that should help, maybe?" she asked, curious about this new, territorial Finn.

He shrugged. "Guess we'll find out."

• • •

He kept her hand in his. He felt more vulnerable now than before he'd claimed her. Touching her seemed to help. So, he kept touching her. He'd only left her to take Oscar to Anders. She needed sleep. He needed her. And Oscar needed a bottle. Anders had taken his son with a wink and a smile. But he'd come back to wake her, to take care of her, and she hadn't been in bed.

He'd panicked.

Watching his scar mar her smooth skin had been a nightmare. It wasn't enough that he'd claimed her, now his mark was on her skin. He wouldn't have blamed her for running. It was the wolf that calmed him down. The wolf knew she'd never leave.

Instead, she'd held him close, let him come apart in her arms, and smiled over the scar. She liked being marked by him. And it filled him with pride to know it.

And shame. He should have told her about the condom, should admit there might be more to worry about. But he couldn't, not yet. Tomorrow, after the moon, he'd lay it all out there and they'd face it together.

"He's gone through like four bottles," Anders said as they walked into the great room.

"Four?" Jessa took Oscar, concerned. She ran her hand across Oscar's forehead and stomach. "Diapers?" Finn followed her, standing at her side, needing her close.

"He's filled a few," Anders added. "It's like he's getting ready for winter or something."

Jessa's gaze flew to his.

"Or something," Dante said.

"We suspected as much." Hollis shrugged. "Theoretically,

it won't hurt him like it does the three of you. He's an infant. His bones aren't fused into place, and he's limber. Yes, he will feel pain, but he'll come through it okay."

Jessa bounced Oscar in her arms, her anxiety reaching him.

"He's eaten considerably more than an infant his age. No throwing up, no excessive bowel movements. And he's been wide awake. I'd say he senses a change coming," Hollis looked at Finn.

Finn's arm slipped around Jessa's waist. "Then we wait and see. You'll stay close?" he asked.

Hollis nodded. "If I'm able."

"I thought... Don't you all change?" Jessa asked.

"Hollis has never been a wolf," Finn said.

She glanced at each of them. "But you said—"

"Oh, he bit all of us," Anders said. "Left Dante here almost without an arm."

He had very few memories of that day. Snippets of the attack. Sounds, tastes, smells... He'd been beyond control. They all had when they'd changed the first time. He'd seen the scar on Dante's arm, knew it had forced Dante's first change to last a week—just so his body could heal.

Finn glanced at Oscar, staring up at Jessa. Would she be safe tonight? Or should he make Hollis watch over Oscar? As much as he wanted to believe Oscar wasn't a threat to Jessa, there were no guarantees. He couldn't risk losing both of them.

"I have a heart arrhythmia. I believe it makes the change dormant," Hollis said. "I carry the infection. My blood is just like theirs under a microscope. Instead of turning into a wolf, I run a fever, suffer chest pain and shortness of breath, throw up blood, pass-out, and generally feel like hell for twenty-four to thirty-six hours."

"Oh." Jessa's sympathy was visible. Finn had to agree. He

wasn't thrilled that he was ruled by the moon, but he thought Hollis had the worst of it. "And if you treat the arrhythmia"

"I change." Hollis shook his head.

"So he has no interest in treating it," Dante said.

"Can you blame him?" Finn asked.

Dante shrugged. "It's not all bad. I'd rather be hunting something down that fainting like a girl." He grinned at Hollis before asking, "Speaking of girls. How are you feeling, Jessa?"

Finn glanced at Dante, noting the smile on his face—and Ander's and Hollis's. He sighed.

"Oh, and, welcome to the family," Anders said. "Glad Finn's decided to keep you. If he didn't, Dante and I were planning to—"

"Stop now." His tone was short and hard.

"I'm glad, too," she said. "Thank you. And thank you for taking care of Oscar. Now, anyone hungry?"

"You shouldn't be cooking," Hollis argued. "You should be resting."

Anders laughed. "Long night?"

Dante grinned. "Guess you still know how to let the wolf take charge after all, eh, Finn?"

"I can cook," Jessa said, her cheeks red.

"May I share?" Hollis asked, glancing between him and Jessa. "It might be useful information if they find a mate."

Finn looked at Jessa. Hollis had a point. Anders and Dante—hell, even Hollis—might want a heads-up that they'd put the one they loved most through agony to claim them. She frowned at him, but Finn nodded.

"The bond between them was cemented by a shared wound," Hollis said.

Anders frowned, and Dante glared at Finn. "What the fuck did you do?" Dante snapped.

Hollis held up his hands. "Nothing. But once they'd... mated...Finn's wound—the one that turned him—appeared on Jessa."

Anders and Dante stared at Jessa.

"No shit?" Anders asked.

Jessa finished adding pasta to the water and held up her shirt. "No shit," she said, smiling at him.

"Did it...did you feel it?" Dante's question was thick. "Or did it just appear?"

Finn stared at the floor, understanding what he was asking. Dante's arm...the pain he'd suffered. How could he do that to someone? Willingly put them through that?

"Jessa?" Hollis asked.

"There was pain," she said, but she didn't add anything. She focused on their dinner.

Fifteen minutes later, they gathered around the large kitchen table. Jessa's mountain of spaghetti and meatballs disappeared rapidly. Conversation was teasing, reminding him just how important these men were to him. They were his friends, yes. But their wolves made them family, a pack he was proud to be a part of. They were here. And for that, he was thankful. All families had their shit.

By the time dinner was over, it was nearing nine. And, as much as he hated to leave them, he wasn't ready to change in front of her.

Oscar was fussing, something he rarely did. Finn could tell Jessa was worried—so was he. But there was nothing he could do. Being so helpless killed him.

"She's waiting this out in your room?" Hollis asked.

Finn nodded.

"I need to clean up," Jessa said, eyeing the dishes.

Finn shook his head. "It'll wait."

He followed Jessa to their room, watching her cradle Oscar in her arms and offer him his bottle. She smiled, so in love with his son that his heart swelled. He lingered, ignoring the prick and pull of change on his skin. He didn't want to leave her. It felt wrong.

"I'll see you soon," he said.

She nodded. "Be safe."

He crossed the room and kissed her, leaving her breathless. "I'm close by." He slipped the medallion off and handed it to her. "Keep it safe for me?"

She nodded.

It took everything he had to leave the room. But keeping her inside, with Oscar, was the only thing that made sense. He wanted to believe that Anders and Dante offered no threat, but they'd never had someone outside the pack there before. Yes, she was his mate, and Oscar was his son, but he wasn't ready to risk their allegiance, or put them in harm's way.

"I'll stay with her," Hollis said. "Oscar?"

"He's going to turn." Finn could feel the energy in his son.

"If I need to separate them?" Hollis asked.

He shook his head. "Whatever it takes, keep them safe."

Hollis nodded and closed the door, locking the deadbolt.

He lingered outside, pacing back and forth. He had to believe they would be safe.

"Come on, Finn," Dante called. "You'll do more good protecting them than worrying over them."

Finn nodded.

"Besides, between Hollis and your pup, I'd say she's got a rock-solid security team." Anders clapped him on the shoulder. "Man, I can't wait to run tonight."

The three of them stripped down. Anders tossed his clothes on the floor while Finn and Dante folded theirs. When they stood on the front porch, Finn welcomed the pull of change. The scent of the pines flooded his nose, along with the winter wind, a distant elk, and the highway miles beyond that. His eyesight sharpened, aided by a million stars and the glow of a perfect white moon.

He gave the others a brief nod and headed into the trees,

the rip and snap of change starting immediately. He fell forward, his hands curling in, nails slicing through the knuckles into long claws. He relaxed, easing the dislocation of his jaw, the lengthening of his bones and teeth, the stretch and tug of his muscles. His skin gave easily, tearing as his thick brown coat covered him from paw to tail. Each vertebra popped into place, his shoulders collapsing in as his chest bowed forward. His senses sharpened, noting each bug and bird, the scents of Anders's and Dante's wolves, the sound of Jessa humming to Oscar inside the cabin.

He swallowed, staring at the orange glow of her window.

His wolf listened to her, aching to go to her. To be with his son.

Instead, he ran, letting his paws carry him to the far perimeter. Anders's wolf greeted him, climbing all over him in eagerness. Finn snapped at him and set off, knowing Anders would follow. They circled the refuge twice before meeting Dante. His greeting was more subdued, but he was happy to be free—to be a wolf—for now.

The refuge wolves were timid, needing time to reacquaint themselves with them, make sure there was no threat. Finn waited until he saw the pack alpha then perked up, throwing back his head to howl his greeting to the others. He was home with his mate and son. And he wanted them all to know it.

Chapter Eleven

Jessa set the bottle on the side table, unable to stop the slight shiver that ran down her spine as another chorus of howls filled the night.

Hollis grinned at her. "It's unnerving."

She nodded. "It's a greeting?" she asked, patting Oscar's back until he gave her a large burp.

"Finn's saying hello." He looked at her.

She smiled, turning her attention to Oscar. He was asleep, his little mouth nursing in his dreams. "I'll let him sleep." She carried him to the crib and laid him down, covering him with a blanket.

"How's the scar?" he asked.

She sat in the rocking chair, ridiculously tired for someone who'd slept most of the day. "I'm fine. Sore, but fine."

"I told Finn it probably wouldn't have happened if he'd used a condom," Hollis sighed.

A condom. She pressed her eyes shut. No condom. They'd been so lost in each other. She swallowed. "Wh-why?"

"I have a theory it's biochemical," Hollis said. "You and

he mixed on a cellular level. I don't think you'll become a wolf—he didn't bite you. But I do think the bond between you was forged because there was no…protection. May I ask a question?"

He didn't *think* she'd become a wolf? Did that mean there was a chance? "I think so," she answered, reeling.

He smiled. "I'm a scientist, Jessa." He leaned forward, steepling his fingers and resting his chin on his thumbs before he asked, "How did it feel? Being bonded? I think I can understand how Finn might feel, considering we're all tied together. But you, as a…non-wolf." He shook his head. "I'm very curious."

"I'm not sure I can explain it adequately. It's like I'm tangled up in him? His thoughts, memories—things I've never felt or heard or seen but are somehow now familiar. And…" She broke off. "I crave him. Even now, when I know he's close, I miss him. Very much. It almost hurts."

Hollis nodded. "The scar?"

She shook her head.

"Pain?" he asked.

She hesitated. "Doctor-patient confidentiality?"

He nodded.

"It was horrible."

"Did it mimic his accident? The puncture?"

"I wasn't there when it happened to him, so I don't know, but it hurt like hell when it happened to me," she said.

"I suspected as much. Sometimes sleep is the only way a body can process pain." He looked at her, then. "Why did you agree?"

"I love him, maybe ever since I walked into his office. I've been drawn to him from the beginning. I belong to him." It was true. "I never imagined he might care for me."

Hollis laughed. "Care for you? We only have glimpses of what he's feeling and thinking. But I assure you, what we've felt is beyond understanding."

She liked the sound of that. She smiled, staring into the fire. "Can I ask you a question?"

He nodded.

"Does it bother you? That you can't change?"

He shrugged. "I've never thought about it. I remember waiting, dreading it along with the others that first time. But seeing what they went through cured me of ever wanting to experience it. I like to be in control."

"And when you're a wolf, you're not?" she asked.

"Not always," he explained. "You're driven by instinct. You're an animal."

An animal. "You're not you?" she asked.

He shrugged. "Finn said it's like being on steroids. His reaction is faster, stronger, less cautious. Instinct rules. He's aware but not always able to stop the wolf from doing things he'd never do."

She couldn't imagine it. Finn was a measured man. His life and his work put him in a place of ultimate control. No wonder he fought the change—and his wolf. At the same time, if Cyrus was coming for them, maybe Finn needed to let his wolf take charge.

The howls started again. "That sounds different." She glanced at Hollis, the surprise on his face drawing her to her feet. "What is it?"

Hollis stood as well, his face hardening. "Mal is here."

"Malachi? Isn't that good?" she asked, curious. Finn would be happy. Even though he'd only mentioned him a few times, it was clear he and Mal had been close, and Finn felt his absence.

Hollis shook his head. "Stay here." He headed for the door.

Maybe it was the look on Hollis's face, or the sudden eerie quiet from outside, but Jessa knew something was very wrong. Oscar must have sensed it, too. His thin wail startled her, breaking off before he cried out with more gusto. She hurried to the crib.

"Oscar," she whispered, staring at the restlessly sleeping baby. But it wasn't the Oscar she knew. In his place was a small gray wolf, curled into a tiny ball. Small ears, small tail, and shiny black nose. "Oh, Oscar." She'd known there was a chance. But... Tears stung her eyes as she gripped the side of the crib.

"He'll be fine, Jessa." Hollis patted her hand. "Let him sleep."

She stared at Oscar, wanting to hold him close. Wolf or not, he was a baby. Her baby. She reached into the crib, stroking thick, soft fur instead of baby-soft skin.

"I need to go make sure Finn and Mal don't kill each other," he said before leaving the room and closing the door behind him.

It took a few minutes for Hollis's words to sink in, but by then he was gone and she was staring at the thick wooden door. "Kill each other?"

Finn and Mal were friends. Finn was his alpha. Wasn't he? She was tired of questions. Of not knowing. But then, she was so new to this world. Finn and his pack were still discovering things, and they'd been this way for ten years.

The wind picked up, carrying the sound of movement outside. The howling started again, breaking off suddenly, followed by a menacing growl. Whatever warm welcome Finn had issued minutes before was gone. The sound of fighting was unmistakable, even to Jessa.

Oscar whimpered, his agitation increasing as the sounds grew louder. He curled tighter, his paws drawn in and his nose buried. She placed her hand on his back, marveling once more at the transformation.

The noises outside grew more fearsome. Surely it wasn't

Finn's pack. It must be the wolves. Maybe they sensed something.

But what?

Last she'd heard, Cyrus and the Others had no idea Finn's pack was here. The only thing they'd had to fear was the moon, and now, that was over.

"It's okay, Oscar." she soothed, hoping she was right. Oscar's heartbeat raced beneath her palm. When she lifted her hand, he whimpered and fussed.

She picked him up, smiling as his wet nose pressed against her collarbone. She wrapped the blanket around him and carried him to the bed. He lay, his eyes barely open, and yawned widely. Even as a wolf pup, he was the most precious baby she'd ever seen. She lay beside him, pulling him close against her stomach and humming softly. She ran her hand down his back in slow, gentle strokes until he eased back into a deep sleep. He was soft and sweet and helpless. He made the same sounds he always did, the same muscle twitches and full body stretches, even if he was no longer human. She rested a hand on his back. As much as it hurt her heart to know this was what his life would be, she couldn't deny she was relieved he'd made the change so easily.

"Sweet dreams, little man," she murmured.

It was silent. Too silent. While Oscar slept easily, she was nervous and on edge. Hollis should have been back by now.

"We're safe," she assured Oscar, assured herself. "Everything's okay."

But the longer they were alone, the more she wondered. What if the Others had found them? Was Cyrus here? Or Thomas? She shook her head. No, Finn would protect them. No matter what, she believed that.

The slight clicking on wood made her stiffen. She hadn't heard the door open, but she tensed, certain she and Oscar were no longer alone. Every instinct told her to move, but where the hell was she supposed to go? Should she run? Take Oscar and hide?

She sat up quickly, her heart in her throat, and came eye to eye with the biggest wolf she had ever seen. Her hands gripped the edge of the bed as she leaned back, digging deep for calm and strength.

The wolf stepped forward, its ears cocked toward her, its eyes fixed on her face. It had the bluest eyes—just like Finn's. She swallowed, her hold easing on the mattress and her heart rate slowing. The wolf stepped forward, a soft whimper rising from his broad chest.

It was Finn.

His blue eyes were unmistakable. The way he looked at her was unmistakable. "Hi," she whispered. He leaned into her, rubbing his face along her jaw, burying his nose in her hair. She wrapped her arms around him, her fear evaporating.

Oscar squeaked, and Finn stepped away from her, his nose scenting the air around Oscar. He cocked his head to the side, a soft whimper in his throat. Jessa lifted the blanket so he could see his son. Finn made an odd noise at the back of his throat, his blue eyes returning to her.

"He's sleeping. He's fine." She marveled at how easy it was to have a one-sided conversation with a wolf—a wolf whose shoulder was bleeding. "Are you okay?" she asked, reaching for him without thought.

He shoved his head under her hand, leaning into her touch with a groan.

She smiled. "I'll take that as a yes." She slid her fingers through the thick, soft fur.

He climbed up beside her, his massive frame dwarfing the bed. He sniffed Oscar, nudging her onto the bed with his nose. She complied, sinking back against the pillows. He waited until she was still then lay across the end of the bed, covering her bare feet with his fur. She looked at him, exhaustion seeping in.

When had this become her life?

What would happen when the real world crept back in?

They had to go back to San Antonio at some point. Her brothers—she was thankful they were oblivious to all this.

In a matter of weeks, her everything had completely changed. She loved this man, this wolf, and his son. Even if the monster hunting them made her blood run cold.

She draped her arm over her eyes, trying to block out the memory of Thomas.

Finn nudged her foot with his nose. He waited until she looked at him then rested his muzzle on his paws, his blue eyes regarding her steadily. She reached out, her fingers sinking into the thick fur of his back, and closed her eyes.

• • •

Finn watched her sleep. He lay, human and naked and wrapped around her, his chin resting on the swell of her hip. He needed to wake her up, to hide her and Oscar before the Others arrived. But he couldn't do it. She was peaceful. No hint of fear or worry troubled her. They had time. When she woke, everything would change—again.

Because of Malachi. Stupid, reckless, arrogant son of a bitch.

He sucked in a deep breath, frustration and anger tempting his wolf. But when he touched Jessa, the contact instantly soothed his need to fight. At least he'd taken a solid hunk out of Mal's haunch—made sure Mal knew who was alpha, no matter how much Mal resented it. If Dante and Anders hadn't jumped in the middle of it—he didn't want to think about that. As mad as he was, he didn't want to kill Mal. But his wolf sure as hell didn't mind teaching him a lesson.

Oscar yawned, his little fist rising into the air as he

stretched in his sleep.

Finn smiled, holding the small hand in his.

No scratches or bruising, no howling or pain—Oscar had slept through his change back from wolf to baby with only a few squeaks. Finn had seen it all. It had been torture. He'd wanted to hold his son but knew Oscar needed space to shift—like he did. And while Finn felt every shift and grind, pop and snap of his son's change, Oscar took it like a champ. "You're strong," he murmured, smiling into his son's heavy-lidded eyes.

Oscar stared at him, instantly alert. He opened his mouth and gurgled. His tiny fingers fastened onto Finn's large finger with a surprisingly sturdy grip.

"That's right, strong," Finn said, resting his chin on Jessa's hip to study his son more closely.

Oscar squealed, his legs kicking out.

Jessa laughed. "Good morning."

Finn kissed her hip, burying his nose in the soft flannel she wore to draw in the comfort he'd need to face the day. If he had it his way, they'd spend the day like this. Wrapped up in each other, discovering this new family he was bound so fiercely to. But since keeping them safe was the only thing that mattered, staying put wasn't an option.

"Morning," he said, his hand sliding underneath the fabric to rest against the skin of her stomach. "You're so damn soft."

"You need a shower. Did you roll in the mud?" she asked, turning onto her back and forcing his hand up to cup her breast. "That wasn't intentional," she murmured, smiling.

But his fingers were already stroking the hard pebble of her nipple. "No complaints." He rose onto one elbow, sliding up her side until they were eye-to-eye.

Jessa's smile faded. "Finn, what happened to you?" Her fingers were feather-light against the gash on his shoulder.

"Malachi," he answered, holding her hand and kissing her

fingertips.

"You need stitches." She tried to pull her hand away.

He grinned at her, cocking an eyebrow. "No stitches." He bent, his lips latching onto her collarbone. He probably should have healed before changing back, but his wolf didn't have fingers and hands, and the urge to touch Jessa had been too great.

"Finn." Her protest was half-hearted.

His fingers worked her nipple until it was a rigid peak. "Are you feeling better?" Because he was so hard he hurt, aching for her. Her breath hitched, her slight nod all permission he needed to unbutton the shirt and suck the tip deep into his mouth. He groaned.

Oscar started to cry.

Finn slumped, releasing her nipple and staring up at her.

Her cheeks were flushed, that hunger in her green eyes almost making him hand Oscar to Hollis. Or Anders. Or Dante. But Malachi was here.

He pushed off the bed and rubbed a hand over his face.

"Are you hungry?" Jessa's cooed to Oscar, her soft voice washed over him. "Did all that wolf business leave you starving?"

He smiled, she didn't seem upset about last night, which was a relief. She'd chosen him, but that didn't mean it would be an easy transition. Watching her scoop up Oscar, her hair spilling over one exposed shoulder, made both his wolf and his heart swell with ownership—and love. He'd never loved like this. Never thought it could exist. Ever. But seeing her with Oscar, watching her smile and laugh filled every missing piece of him with happiness. And it scared the shit out of him. He hadn't been happy in a long time, and he'd been fine. Good, even. For the first time in years, he had something to lose.

She and Oscar could be taken away from him.

"Jessa." He stood. "I'm going to get some breakfast started. Come out when he, and you, are dressed."

"Might take your own advice," she teased, eyeing his nakedness with open appreciation.

He shook his head. "You're killing me." He loved seeing her look at him that way, wanting him the way he wanted her.

"You started it," she said, the hitch in her voice having an immediate effect on his body. He heard her sharp inhale. "Here," she said, offering him the medallion.

"I'd like to finish it," he said, closing the distance between them to kiss her, hard. "But it'll wait." He slid on the medallion, tugged on some pajama pants, and left her, not caring that the dirt and blood from the night before still caked his bare skin.

Hollis sprawled in the large chair before the fire, dozing.

Dante gripped a massive cup of coffee, bleary-eyed and brooding.

"Hey," Anders said, digging through the large refrigerator. "Man, I'm starved." Finn nodded. The morning after was all about refueling—and sleep. Not that any of them were likely to be getting a lot of sleep for a while.

"Pancakes? Or French Toast?" Anders asked.

"Both," Dante sounded off.

Anders nodded.

Malachi came in then, rubbing a towel over his shaggy brown hair. "Long as I don't have to cook it," he said. He looked at Finn, a mix of anger and hurt and reluctant obedience settling on his features. Then his eyes went wide.

"I'll cook." Jessa's voice. "Can you feed him?" she asked, holding Oscar toward Finn.

He took his son, but his gaze never left Mal.

Mal was staring at Oscar, studying him. Finn saw the sadness, the slight tightening around Mal's eyes, heard the harsh clearing of his throat. But when he looked at Finn, his smile finally reached his eyes. "He's a good-looking boy." He moved closer, stooping to look at Oscar.

Oscar stared up at Mal, all blue eyes and curiosity.

"I don't mind cooking," Anders said.

"Neither do I," Jessa argued. "And I don't particularly like being useless."

Anders snorted. "The kitchen is yours."

She laughed, the sound putting an instant smile on Finn's face.

Mal's blatant interest in Finn's reaction was hard to miss. His brow cocked before he turned his attention to Jessa. "You must be Mrs. Alpha?" It was a head-to-toe inspection, the kind that Finn barely tolerated. When he was done, he nodded, glancing back at Finn.

Jessa looked at Mal, her smile dimming as she glanced between them. "Malachi?" She held her hand out. "Jessa Talbot."

"Mrs. Alpha," Anders said, sitting on one of the bar stools.

Finn watched color stain Jessa's cheek. Her green gaze met his, the warmth waiting for him drawing him close. "Suits me," he murmured.

Hollis stumbled into the kitchen then. "I smell coffee." Jessa poured him a cup, putting it into Hollis's hands before he knew it. "Thanks," he mumbled. He looked weak, obviously the sickness took far longer to recover from than the change. "What's the plan? Who's taking Oscar? And Jessa? What did I miss?"

Finn glared at Hollis. It would be nice to make it through breakfast before talk of the Others and reinforcements came into play.

"You've got to get them out of here, Finn," Anders said. "Last night was hard on us all."

Jessa paused mid-stir. "What happened last night? I thought it was safe?"

Finn nodded. "It is, for now."

"The Others caught a scent trail," Dante explained, still staring into his coffee. "Won't take them long to find us."

"We can't keep running." Mal's anger was evident. "I'm tired of this shit. I'm tired of always being on the move, looking over my shoulder."

Finn watched Jessa's reaction. She frowned, mixing the pancake batter with renewed vigor.

"I won't put them in harm's way." Finn kept his voice low, but the threat was real. "I know you want to fight, Mal, but I won't risk Oscar and Jessa."

"So we wait?" Mal glanced at Oscar. "Until they get him—"

"They won't." Jessa set the bowl on the counter and took Oscar from his arms.

Finn stepped closer, sliding an arm around her shoulders and pressing a kiss to her temple. "They won't," he said against her ear.

Mal held his hands up. "You can't be serious?"

"Jesus, Mal, enough," Dante snapped.

"You think sparing her the truth will change it? Cara? Phillip and Annie? Brown's family?" His rage was barely in check. "Mine?"

"So the plan is to scare the shit out of her?" Anders asked.

"She should be scared," Mal argued. "But *we* shouldn't be. We're stronger than they are. We can take them down—one by one if we have to. This waiting for them has to fucking stop."

"Enough." The word tore from Finn's lips, more growled than spoken.

Silence.

But Mal's words hung there, choking Finn. They would come for Oscar. Or Jessa. Could he expect them to keep running? That was no life for any of them. He stared at her, wanting to run, to hide her away someplace safe. What was safe? Where could he take them that the Others wouldn't eventually find?

Jessa bounced Oscar in her arms, her green eyes seeking his as she crossed the room to sit before the fire. Oscar's fist tangled in her hair, pulling her focus back to his son. While his heart thundered in his chest, her graceful movements revealed none of her fear. She was brave but fragile—in need of protection. His protection. And his pack.

The wolf wanted to fight, to stand their ground. But he'd spent too much time avoiding his wolf and the instincts that drove him. Turning that off would be a challenge. His hand slid up, grasping the silver medallion he'd worn for almost ten years. It had been his compass, warning him when he teetered too close to his wild side. If he was going forward with this, entertaining Mal's idea, he had no business wearing it.

He paced the room, glaring at Mal, looking to Dante and Anders for some insight. How did they feel? He was their alpha, but this was too big a decision to make on his own.

Hollis carried a newly made bottle to Jessa, offering it to her without a sound.

"Thank you," she said, smiling up at Hollis.

Finn studied her, the curve of her smile as she lay Oscar on her knees, speaking to him in a soft, adoring tone. Nothing could happen to them—he had to make sure of that. "How many?" Finn asked.

"Small group." Mal shrugged. "Cyrus wasn't with them."

That was good. "How long?" Finn asked.

Mal looked at him "Maybe two days."

"*Small* group?" Dante asked, his interest piqued.

"Maybe eight," Mal said.

"Hell, we can take eight," Anders said, snorting and taking over breakfast. "That's nothing."

Jessa glanced at him then back at Oscar.

"What about them?" Hollis asked. "Mal is right. Their presence causes a definite disadvantage."

Finn paced again, his heart twisting at the options that

spun in his mind.

"If you're thinking what I think you're thinking, they can't be together," Dante said.

Anders nodded. "Talk about a clear target."

Finn nodded. No matter which way he went, he wasn't happy. The thought of taking Oscar from Jessa was a punch to the gut. He was her baby, Finn knew that. But what choice did he have? Even though the dumb shit had brought trouble to his door, Mal was right. No more running. The whole intimidation tactic had to end, here and now. "I'll call Brown. He can take Jessa." He didn't look at her, couldn't look at her. "Hollis, your moon-sickness over? You'll take Oscar. The rest of us will wait for the Others here," Finn said, staring around the room at the men he considered his family.

"'Bout damn time," Mal said, rubbing his hands together.

Finn didn't deny the flare of anticipation that set the hairs on the back of his neck straight.

"Excuse me," Jessa said, handing Oscar to Hollis and leaving the room.

He followed, pushing the bedroom door closed behind him.

She stared at him, hurt and angry—and silent.

"Be mad at me after you're gone," he said, pulling her into his arms. "Right now, I need you." His lips latched onto her neck, his hands stripping the clothes from her body. When he was buried deep inside her, he felt better. This separation was temporary. And it was for the best. He took his time making love to her, his fingers and hands and mouth driving her wild. He studied her reactions, her sounds, the bowing of her body. Whatever it took, he would protect this—he would protect her.

His wolf knew how to kill. It was in his blood. Finn would murder every last one of them so that, maybe, he'd never have to do it again.

Chapter Twelve

Jessa stared at the starless sky, toying with Finn's medallion around her neck. She stood by the large window of the motel Brown had found for them on the San Francisco Bay, unable to enjoy the view. They hadn't heard from Finn in five days. She'd seen Oscar via Facetime and Skype, but she ached to hold him in her arms. Not to mention her brothers. Harry was getting suspicious, but she'd done her best to make it sound like they'd extended their holiday—not gone into hiding. She missed them, missed home, so much.

"Got you some dinner, Miss Talbot." Brown placed a wrapped sandwich on the table. "You need to eat something, ma'am."

She unwrapped the paper and nibbled on the bread.

"I'll be next door," Brown said.

She nodded. "Thank you."

He left, closing the door to the adjoining room softly. It was unlocked, in case she needed him. But what could one man do against a werewolf? She'd asked him, and the answer hadn't been reassuring.

"They don't go down easily," Brown had said. "You have to shoot them straight in the heart. Or in the head. But I've had bullets bounce off their skulls."

"Thick-headed," she'd murmured. "What about the whole silver thing?"

He nodded. "It works, but you still need to be a crack-shot. If you don't get the brain or heart, you're just pissing them off. Silver makes them sick and it prevents them from being able to change into a wolf, so it can be useful." He seemed to realize he might have shared too much information and offered her his pistol. "This would be too big for you, too much kick. But Mr. Dean should get you outfitted—and trained—just in case."

She'd never been one to read high-concept fiction or watch supernatural movies. Life was life—there was enough conflict without adding things that didn't exist. But now she wished she'd paid more attention. The few movies she'd managed to watch in her hotel room had been horrible. For one thing, the werewolf was always some crazed monster bent on murdering and disemboweling people. For another, no one survived.

Each night, she cried herself to sleep and tried to forget what Finn might be up against, and how much she missed Oscar. If separating them would make him safer, slow down the Others, Jessa wasn't about to argue. His safety came first.

It was reassuring to see how Oscar took to Hollis. Hollis's calm nature probably had something to do with it. She had no idea where they were, but she knew he was safe and well cared for. And that, for now, was enough. It had to be.

The last few days they'd flown in a strange series of loops and layovers before renting a car and traveling through San Francisco, north to Mendocino, a bustling wine and arts community. Brown had checked them into a small motel on the outskirts of town. She had a view of the bay and not much else. Instead of being caught up in the beauty of her surroundings, she was lonely and worried.

She'd skimmed a novel and watched the news, but she was too wide awake to consider sleeping. A long shower helped, even if the hot water had run out. She brushed out her hair and slipped into the shirt she'd stolen from Finn. She wrapped her arms around herself and buried her nose against the sleeve, but it didn't smell like Finn anymore.

She paced the room, so restless she wanted to scream. She slid the balcony door open, knowing she was breaking Brown's rules and not caring. She needed fresh air. She needed to stop feeling so damn trapped. She stood, sucking cold air deep into her lungs, fighting back frustrated tears.

"Jessa?"

She froze, peering into the dark below her. In that instant, she felt pure terror. Her fingers tightened around the bannister before she pushed off, stepping into the shadows and hoping she hadn't just sentenced both herself and Brown to a painful death.

"Jessa?"

She knew that voice and responded to it instantly. "Finn?"

He was moving toward the door. She spun and went inside, running to meet him.

He met her on the stairwell, shoving her against the wall as his mouth found hers. She gripped his hair, tugging him close, devouring his kiss, his mouth, his tongue. She swayed into him, but he caught her. "You're safe. Oscar is safe," he whispered against her lips.

She lost herself in the feel of his hands and mouth, his taste and smell. Her head fell back as he nipped her neck, dropping hot, wet kisses all the way to her ear. He sucked her earlobe into his mouth, his teeth making her shudder. He inhaled, the groan that tore from deep in his throat making her tighten with want.

He gripped her hips, lifting her off her feet to carry her inside. She wrapped her legs around his waist, holding on to him. He carried her up the stairs. When they stumbled into her room, he kicked the door shut and pressed her against thick wood, his lips merciless and hungry. She wanted more— all of him. She needed him.

Her hands slid between them, unfastening his pants and pushing them open.

"Wait," he said, pulling a condom from his pocket, tearing the packet, and rolling it on. He kissed her, pinning her to the door with his arms as he thrust into her.

The noise he made. The look on his face—raw, desperate, vulnerable. She couldn't breathe. Her heart tripped over itself and her lungs constricted. She watched the muscle in his jaw bulge, his nostrils flare, watched the heat in his eyes as they bored into hers. As he bored into her.

"I missed you," she whispered, turning into his kiss. "Oh, God, Finn."

His hold tightened, almost bruising. His hands eased, but the yearning in his eyes told her the truth. He needed her touch just as much as she needed his. She arched into him, moaning as he slid deep.

"Jessa," he ground out, crushing her against his chest and spinning them.

In seconds, she was on the bed.

He was stripping, tossing his clothes hurriedly.

She sat up, watching, waiting. When he was naked, she frowned. His body was covered in deep bruising, several wide scratches scouring his right side. "Finn—"

He shook his head, tugging her shirt off. His hand cupped her breast, his thumb raking over its peak.

She lay back, stretching her arms over her head to grip the far edge of the mattress.

He crawled onto the bed, his tongue licking the sensitive

spot behind her knee, his mouth sucking her soft inner thigh. The sweep of his tongue against her tight, aching nub was too much. A few strokes and she was out of her mind. Two fingers slid inside her, teasing, working her into a frenzy. His tongue was magic, his mouth demanding her submission. She surrendered, her body bowing off the bed, tightening with the power of her climax.

His lips traveled up, over her hip, lingering over her scar before latching onto her nipple. His lips traveled up the swell of her shoulder, silky neck, slender throat and jaw. His tongue slid into her mouth as he pushed inside of her. A shudder racked his body, rock-hard as he slammed into her. His hands gripped the edge of the mattress, covering hers and pinning her in place. Pure sensation swept her away. She was lost in his blue eyes at the urgency of each thrust. Her release crashed over her, her scream broken and hoarse.

Watching him come apart, the incredible strain on his face as he powered into her, took her breath away. The sound of his growl, his hands gripping hers as he came, was incredibly empowering.

When he rolled onto his back, he pulled her against him. His arms were steel bands, holding her tightly. She placed a hand on his chest, stroking the place over his thundering heart and burying her face against his side.

It was enough for now that he was here, safe in her arms. Any questions she had could wait.

"Jessa."

She looked up at him.

His hand smoothed the hair from her face, his eyes exploring every feature.

"What is it?" she asked, smiling.

He shook his head. "I want to look at you."

"You missed me?" she asked.

He arched a brow, his jaw clenching tightly before he

managed, "You could say that."

Her attention wandered to the scratches. She traced four fingers along the ridges. Claw marks, and several puncture marks on his forearm. She sat up, her attention wandering along his thighs. "Stitches?" she asked, looking at him.

But he was too busy staring at her, and the tenderness on his face made her ache.

"Finn," she whispered, watching the shift of emotion on his features. Whatever he was thinking, he seemed at a loss to express it.

"What happened?" she asked, scooting closer and taking his hands in hers.

His gaze locked with hers. "We killed them."

Her chest hurt.

"*I* killed them," he clarified.

Jessa didn't know what to say. Her heart was lodged in her throat.

"Mal was scouting. Anders and Dante were still inside." He ran a hand over his face. "I saw them… They asked where Oscar was. Where you were. Said things that made my blood boil. I saw red. The wolf…" He broke off.

Her hands tightened around him. "Mal said there were eight of them?"

He shook his head, his attention shifting to their hands. "Seven."

She swallowed. He fought them alone? "And Anders… Dante… Surely they heard—"

"They showed up but…" He couldn't look her in the eye. "It was already over." He wasn't proud. He seemed almost ashamed.

"You did what you had to do," she said softly.

He looked at her, then. "Did I?"

She cradled his face in her hands. "You protected your pack, Finn. And I love you for it."

• • •

He hadn't meant to tell her. But somehow it all came tumbling out. He'd killed seven men and he hadn't felt a single ounce of regret. Not until it was over. But seeing her now, hearing her say she loved him… Right or wrong, he'd kill them again if it silenced a threat against her or Oscar.

He'd tried to talk to them, to buy some time, but they were there for one reason—to taunt him. And they had. The things they said they'd do to Jessa, how they'd turn her into one of their pack or use her until they were done. And Oscar? They'd called him a chew toy, one they'd make squeak and bleed.

He pulled his hands from hers and slipped from the bed.

"Cyrus wasn't there?" she asked.

He shook his head.

"What do we do now?" she asked.

He glanced at her. "We hope they get the message."

She nodded, coming to stand by his side. "Does it hurt?" she asked, running her fingers along the gouge on his buttock.

He turned, looking down at her. "Nothing hurt as much as being away from you."

"I was so worried," her voice broke. "Terrible nightmares—"

He tugged her against him, kissing her deeply. He knew all about nightmares. Every fucking night he relived the Others' words, saw their threat come to life…and there was nothing he could do about it. He'd seen Jessa as a wolf—at Cyrus's side—and Oscar's bed full of blood.

"Dreams," he said against her mouth. "Just dreams."

She nodded, her fingers sliding into his hair. "You're here."

"I'm here," he repeated. He'd traveled all night to get to her, and he wasn't letting her out of his sight.

Having her take the lead was completely unexpected, and hot as hell. Soft lips latched onto his, tugging his lower lip into her mouth. The nip and tug of her teeth, the breathy moan in the back of her throat, the bite of her nails on his shoulders—her hunger was all it took to make him rock-hard and aching.

The sweep of her hair fell against his shoulder, surrounding him in her scent. There was no place he'd rather be. He'd missed everything about her. The urge to touch her, to hold her close, to bury himself inside her until there was no fear of ever losing her again was all-consuming.

Her hands slid down his chest, gripping his hand in hers and bringing it between her legs. "Love me. Don't stop."

"I'll never stop," he growled. Whatever she wanted, he'd give her. His fingers slid over the nub at her core. He worked her over, stroking and teasing until she was shuddering around him. She clamped down on him—her muscles contracting. When she came, arching into his hand, his wolf wanted to howl in satisfaction.

They made it back to the bed, falling into the blankets before he was rolling on a condom from the bedside table. Her fingers slid along his engorged shaft and back to the tip, tracing the sensitive head as she pressed an open-mouthed kiss to his chest. "Damn. It." The words tore from his throat. While he sucked her earlobe into his mouth, his thumb stroked her inflamed flesh relentlessly. His other hand slid around her waist, gripping her buttocks and lifting her to take him.

But she pushed him back onto the mattress. He stared up at her, mesmerized by the raw hunger on her face. "You're so damn beautiful," he murmured. And she was his. His heart thumped, full of so much more than lust.

When she bent forward, her long blond hair slipped across his stomach. The shock of her lips closing on the tip of his erection, her tongue teasing the crown, stole his breath. His body jerked up, forcing him deeper into the wet heat of her mouth. She moaned, sending shockwaves along his shaft. It was good. Too good. But he wanted more than his own pleasure. And dammit, he had to touch her.

"Jessa," he whispered, pulling her up and cradling her face in his hands. Forehead to forehead, he wrapped her close and breathed her in.

"I missed you," she whispered. "So much." Green eyes bore into his as she smiled. He groaned, burying his face in the hollow between her breasts as she lowered herself onto him. Control slipping, he wound his arms around her waist to keep their rhythm maddeningly slow and steady.

Stroking, cupping, biting, licking, he explored every inch of her. No matter how he took her, her body offered endless temptation. Making her cry out, her body twitching and rising, only heightened his craving. He knew she was worn out, her body consumed by the same endless longing. Sweat slicked them both, but he couldn't get enough.

"Jessa," his voice was gruff as he let go of his restraint. His hands rested on her thighs, caressing the silky-soft skin as he watched the play of sensation on her face. So damn beautiful. "Let go."

She stiffened instantly, her release rolling over her with a broken cry. He pumped into her, then, holding her in place until he came with a growl. They were gasping when she slumped forward over him, her hair falling around his shoulders and her cheek resting against his chest.

Nothing eased his wolf like holding her. The wolf would be happy to stay that way—until he wanted her again.

"I can't move," she gasped.

"Then don't," he murmured, pressing a kiss against her forehead.

She relaxed then, her breathing slowly easing as his fingers traced the length of her spine. "When will we leave?" she asked.

"Soon," he answered.

"I miss him," she said, a completely different type of longing in her voice.

He hugged her close, rolling her beneath him. "Do you want to leave now?"

"I don't think I can walk," she answered, looking exhausted—but happy.

"Are you complaining?" he asked, nuzzling her nipple.

"Are you trying to kill me?" she asked.

But all he saw was her nipple, tight and hard and demanding his attention. "You want me."

She looked at him. "Yes. But I need to see Oscar."

"Your son?" he asked, watching the love in her smile.

She nodded.

"Then let's go." He pushed off the bed, groaning at the vision she made. Her body was flushed, bearing several patches of darkened skin where he'd sucked too hard too long. And damn, but he'd do it again. Her hair was a mess, and she looked beautiful. "One more time?"

She shook her head, her eyes going wide. "Seriously?"

He looked down at the evidence of his arousal. "Seriously."

She sat up, her hand clasping him—

"Mr. Dean?" Brown called through the door. "You have a phone call."

Jessa jumped back, burrowing under the covers. Finn laughed. "Coming," he answered.

Jessa threw a pillow at him. "You take your phone call. I'll take a shower—"

"What if I like you all sweaty and smelling like me?"

Her cheeks were red, but she looked him in the eye and said, "Then you'll have to do it again, later."

He tugged up his boxers. "Deal." Then he headed through the connecting door into Brown's room.

"It's Hollis," Brown said, offering him the phone.

"Where is your phone?" Hollis snapped.

"In Jessa's room. Why?" he snapped back. "What's wrong?"

"Is it charged?" Hollis sighed. "Never mind. You need to move. Now. Cyrus has been spotted in San Francisco. He's with two others, a man and a woman. From the looks of it, the woman might be Brown's daughter. Tess Brown was the name used to rent a car."

He ran a hand over his head. Brown's daughter was with the Others. She'd have to be if she was still alive. But how would Brown take the news that his daughter was a werewolf? And she was coming, tracking Jessa. Brown was a professional, ex-military, never questioning orders and loyal to Finn. But this was his daughter—the whole reason he'd stayed with Finn and his pack. "We'll leave. Any other movement?"

"They're in San Antonio," Hollis broke off. "There was a break-in at the Talbot house. The place was searched and ripped apart."

Finn sat, his knees going out. "Are her brothers okay?" Jessa would never forgive him if her brothers were infected.

"No contact has been made. Gentry is installing some audio and video feeds on the premises."

Gentry was a friend of Brown's, also ex-military. Where Brown had a personal reason for remaining loyal to Finn and his pack, Gentry enjoyed the steady paycheck, the intrigue, and the occasional adrenaline rush that came with his work. Finn appreciated his attention to detail. "Let me know what he finds." Jessa's family didn't deserve to be sucked into this shit.

Unease twisted his gut. Dammit.

He stood. "I'll head there now." If the Others were sniffing around San Antonio, Jessa and Oscar shouldn't go there. "Take Oscar to the safe house in Maine. I'll send Brown and Jessa to meet you there. Anders and Dante, too. I'll get Mal to come with me." At least Jessa would be with Oscar again. That would ease his mind.

"Got it. Find your phone," Hollis snapped before hanging up.

"I'm taking Miss Talbot to Maine?" Brown asked.

Finn stared at him. He had a choice to make. "Yes," he said. "We have a tail."

Brown's gray eyes met his. "Cyrus?"

Finn nodded.

Brown cleared his throat and nodded. "I'll plot the route carefully." Brown was a master at helping Finn get lost. It was a skill he was beginning to truly appreciate.

"He's traveling with a man. And a woman." Finn waited, watching Brown's face. "It might be your daughter."

Shock and horror first. Then anger, followed by sadness and grief. "She's one of them?" Anger took precedence in the end.

"We don't know," he said. "Tess Brown was the name used to rent a car."

"Tess?" His voice broke. "Tess's my...baby girl." He shook his head, but his expression remained the same, guarded. His hands flexed, fisted, and flexed again.

"Can you do this?" Finn asked, hurting for the man he also considered his friend. "If you can't, I'll call in someone else. I need to protect Jessa."

Brown nodded once.

"Are you sure? I can—"

"Have I ever let you down?" Brown asked, turning steely eyes upon him.

"Never."

Brown nodded. "No plans to start now."

Finn clapped the man's shoulder and headed back through the connecting door. Telling Brown about his daughter was one thing. Telling Jessa the Others had tossed her home was another.

He lingered inside the door, watching as she dried her hair with a thick white towel. She'd slipped into white leggings and a brightly colored shirt that read "I left my Heart in San Francisco."

"Nice shirt," he said, crossing to her side.

She wrinkled her nose at him. "Brown likes the grab and go style of shopping. He grabs, we go."

Finn smiled, leaning against the counter to stare at her.

She paused. "Is everything okay?"

"It will be," he assured her. "But you need to go now."

"Me? Not we?" She waited. "Tell me."

"I need to go back to San Antonio." He'd promised to keep her family safe. He wasn't going to fail. "There was a break-in at your place—"

"My brothers?"

"Are safe," he assured her. "But I don't want you and Oscar there. Not now."

She nodded slowly, but what she said was "I'm coming, too."

"No, you're not." He gripped her shoulders.

"Finn... My brothers." She stared at him.

"Are fine, Jessa. I promise you. Our son needs you. Please. Go with Brown." He pulled her close. "I need to know you're safe."

"I miss them, Finn." A tear fell down her cheek, breaking his heart and infuriating the wolf. As far as the wolf was concerned, his job was to make Jessa happy. Her tears didn't sit well. "Where am I going?"

"A safe house. We have several. If we're caught out on a full moon, we can lock ourselves in. Prevent attacks." He spoke softly, his hand cupping her cheek. "The same reason for the safe room in the apartment." She wasn't listening anymore. How could she? Her whole life had been about caring for her brothers, and now he was keeping her from them.

She shook her head, closing her eyes. "Safe houses and attacks." She sniffed. "Full moons." Her voice broke. "Wolves. Bonds. Packs…" She was sobbing now. "What I wouldn't give for a night of crappy delivery pizza, an old movie, and… and sleep."

He pulled her against him. "I'm sorry Jessa." She continued to sob, her body quaking in his arms. "When this is over, I promise I'll give you whatever you want." When this was over. He just had to finish it. He had to.

"Are we ready?" Brown came in but stopped on the threshold when he saw them. "Apologies," he murmured.

Jessa pushed away from Finn. "I'm ready."

Finn reached for her, but she was crossing the room, her eyes glued to the floor at her feet.

"We'll drive into Oregon and fly out." Brown told him the route they'd take. It would take eighteen hours, give or take layovers.

Finn nodded. "Check in at Houston," he replied, his eyes never leaving Jessa's. "I'll be there as soon as I can."

"Will do," Brown agreed, opening the door and peering outside.

Finn couldn't leave it this way. She was in his arms before she could argue, his thumb forcing her head back to look at him. "I love you, Jessa. I'll see you soon."

Her chin quivered, more tears spilling over as he pressed a hard kiss against her lips. "Hurry, Finn," she whispered as he walked out the door.

Chapter Thirteen

Jessa stared at the wall of pregnancy tests, hoping to hell she was wrong. It was too soon, wasn't it? She had every reason to be an emotional mess without being pregnant. Falling in love was enough to make a person super-sensitive. Throw in the whole werewolf thing, pack rivalry, running for your life, and simple exhaustion was a reasonable explanation for what ailed her.

At least, she hoped that was the case.

Brown didn't say a thing when she bought it. She placed the test on the counter. He occupied himself outside the ladies' room, reading an outdoor magazine, while she paced the drugstore's tile lined floor until three-minutes were up.

A bright blue plus sign.

She frowned, sitting on the toilet in shock. It had to be wrong. It had to be. *Please let it be wrong.* But the only way to know was try again.

"Mr. Brown," she asked through the door. "I need another one."

Mr. Brown returned minutes later with another test.

She stacked the pregnancy tests side by side, promptly bursting into tears when the second bright blue plus sign appeared.

"Miss Talbot?" Mr. Brown knocked on the door. "Are you all right?"

Her wailed, "Fine," wasn't convincing. And seconds later, Brown stood inside the small woman's restroom, glancing from her to the tests.

She didn't bother asking how he picked the lock. Or argue with him when he tucked both tests into the plastic bag containing her latest wardrobe change. No, he offered her his hand and led her from the bathroom without a word.

When they were headed north on highway seventy, he asked. "What can I do for you Miss Talbot?"

She glanced at the man. "Can you tell me about Cara, Mr. Brown?"

He was quiet.

"Please," she pushed. "More specifically, how much time passed between Finn's… involvement with her and Oscar's birth?"

Mr. Brown cleared his throat. "No more than six months, I believe."

She nodded. She'd have to google a wolf's gestation cycle when she had the chance. Or talk to Hollis. Chances were this wouldn't be a run-of-the-mill pregnancy. Why would it be? For an hour, she stared out the window, aware of trees, snow, and winding roads. No traffic this time of the morning, most of the world was still asleep. And silence. She jumped when Mr. Brown murmured, "We're almost to the airfield."

If that was supposed to be comforting, it wasn't. "Airfield?"

"Better to puddle jump in a smaller plane than attempt travel through a large airport. Too many eyes."

She rested her head against the headrest. "Mr. Brown, what did you do before all of this?"

"I was a Navy SEAL, Miss Talbot."

She nodded. "I suppose there's always some sort of fight or conflict surrounding Finn." Poor Finn. What would he do when he found out about the baby? She covered her face with her hands. A baby that would be like Oscar...

Panic pressed in on her, so she focused on the sound of Brown's voice.

"Until last month, Mr. Dean's life was fairly mundane. We knew of the Others's existence, had seen what they were capable after they attacked Mal, but they tended to stay on the sidelines where Mr. Dean was concerned. More like they were watching him, studying him."

She glanced his way. "Studying him?"

"Best way to understand your opponent—determine what their next move is." He nodded. "Mr. Dean's very good at being unpredictable. I'm sure he frustrated the hell out them."

She smiled. "Good."

Mr. Brown smiled, too.

"Why do you work for him?" she asked. "If you don't mind my asking, that is?"

"Mr. Dean and Mr. Robbins—"

"Mr. Robbins?"

"Hollis," he clarified. "They saved my life. And they gave me a reason to live after I lost my family."

"I'm so—" Her words were cut short as their rental truck was rammed. Jessa had no time to think or brace, only hold on as the vehicle went spinning across the highway into oncoming traffic.

Her head smacked the passenger side window, leaving her ears ringing and a hot throb in her temple.

"Miss Talbot?" Mr. Brown's voice was firm. "Can you move?"

She hung, upside down, the blood rushing to her head,

and she promptly threw up.

"I'm unbuckling you," Mr. Brown said, his hands working the seat belt clasp and releasing her.

It wasn't far to go—the truck cab had collapsed.

"Light it?" A woman's voice. Outside.

A man spoke, irritated. "Give them a minute."

Jessa glanced at Brown. He'd pulled his gun from the holster under his jacket. "Can you move?" he whispered softly.

"Others?" she asked.

He nodded.

"I can move," she whispered.

"Take this." He shoved a second gun into her hands. "Let me go out first, then follow me, out your window."

"I'm lighting it," the woman argued.

"Maybe they're dead." The man sounded hopeful.

"They're not dead," another voice, one she knew. One that left her cold and quaking with fear. "We need to make sure."

"Cyrus," she whispered.

Brown's jaw clenched, his eyes narrowing slightly. "Ready?"

No, she wasn't ready. But Brown was out the window before she could answer, and the noises that followed didn't offer much comfort. She scrambled out her window, wincing as broken glass cut through the back of her shirt and embedded in her palms. By the time she was on her feet, Brown had shot one man and was staring at the woman—gun ready.

"Can you do it, Mr. Brown?" Cyrus's voice was taunting.

Jessa huddled behind the truck, bracing her shaking arm on the bent metal frame of the vehicle they'd been driving. She wiped the wetness from her face, rubbed it on her white leggings. She gripped the gun in her hand, but her arm was shaking, going numb.

Brown's arm fell, dropping to his knees in defeat.

"The weakness of humanity," Cyrus said. "Now, watch her do what you couldn't. Tess."

The woman was staring at her, eyes narrowed, a small smile on her face. The sort of smile that caused fear to churn in the pit of her stomach.

Cyrus grabbed Brown by the hair, forcing the man to turn—to see her. "Run Jessa," Brown called out.

That was when Jessa saw the gun in the woman's hand. She pushed off the car, swaying on unsteady legs. Walking wasn't easy, running was almost impossible. She tried to make it off the road and into the woods. Maybe in the trees, she could lose them.

The gun went off, and Jessa was knocked forward, a shooting pain in her right shoulder. Two more shots and she was on the ground, her nose buried in wet leaves and dirt. She couldn't move, her limbs were too heavy...

"You killed one of mine. I killed one of yours," Cyrus's voice rang out. "You tell Mr. Dean what happened here. You tell him I shot her in the back and she died in the dirt. Tell him I'll be waiting."

Cyrus's words echoed in her ears. This was all to get Finn. All of it.

"If he doesn't come, his pup is next," Cyrus continued.

Jessa sobbed, an odd numbness seeping into her limbs and weighing her down. She hurt, yes, but it was dull—fading.

She didn't want to die. She didn't want to leave Finn or Oscar. Or the baby their love had made. Breathing became difficult, her vision blurred...

"Jessa Talbot," Cyrus said, lifting her easily into his arms. He sniffed her temple, his cold eyes narrowing. "You smell different now." He sniffed again, bending close to her. "Plus one?" His smile grew. "I have to give it to him. Mating is a more exciting way to build a pack than biting."

"Am I going to die?" she forced the words through stiff lips.

He held her away from him. "Now? No. Tranquilizer darts. I still need you." His hand tilted her head back, his pale eyes searching hers. "Until this pup is born, that is. After that, I might decide to keep you as a pet. Or I'll kill you." He frowned then. "You're bleeding. Let's wrap this up so you can rest more comfortably."

He carried her back to the street as a black SUV pulled up and two men climbed out, immediately going through the wreckage. It was hard to keep her eyes open now but she tried. She had no idea what they were looking for.

They dumped the contents of her purse on the road, shredding the fabric and tossing it carelessly. They found the shopping bag and the pregnancy tests.

He held his hand out, taking one of the tests. "Leave the other one in plain sight," he said.

She started crying when she saw Brown, his head bashed and bloody.

"He's alive, Jessa." Cyrus said. "He needs to stay alive."

She glanced at him, torn between tears and fury.

He smiled down at her. "Miss Talbot, let me make one thing clear. Until this pup is born, I will treat you generously. But never mistake my patience with tolerance." He sighed. "You may disagree with my manner of doing things. You may feel anger, or fear, for me. But I will not tolerate disrespect. So, when you're feeling especially annoyed, I recommend you keep your eyes on the ground. Or I will feel obligated to discipline you." He gripped her chin with one hand. "And while I know I would enjoy your lessons, you, I promise, would not."

Jessa closed her eyes, unable to fight the darkness creeping in.

"Sleep now, Jessa," his voice was low, almost sympathetic.

"You'll need your energy."

• • •

"We can take 'em," Mal said, pacing the rooftop.

"Her brother is inside." Finn ran a hand through his hair, exhaustion weighing him down.

"You were right about one thing." Mal smiled at him. "Mates and kids, man. Talk about complicating things."

Finn smiled, he had no choice.

"Guess the real question is, is all this shit worth it?" Mal paced.

"Yes."

"Don't think about it or anything. Just say the first thing that comes to mind." Mal frowned at him. "I'm serious, Finn. You don't have to be all loyal wolf-man daddy to me."

Finn shook his head. "I don't need to think about it. Jesus, Mal. They're mine."

Mal was staring at him. "And the plan? We sit here and watch Gentry shoot Thomas through the window? How the hell are you going to explain that to her brother? I'm thinking that might lead to questions we're trying to avoid."

"No." He sighed. Mal was so ready for a fight he didn't hear anything he didn't want to. "I go in," he repeated. "Gentry will cover me, yes, but he said it's only Thomas inside. We have to trust his intel. Give me five minutes and follow me in."

He nodded. "Let's do it."

Finn's gaze swept the street again. No cars parked, no suspicious movements. Was Thomas going rogue? What was his plan here? "I want this done, clean and easy." He glanced at his watch. They'd been inside a half hour, tops. He was pissed that Harry had come home without his driver—but the kid didn't get how serious the situation was. And while he hoped Harry hadn't been infected, he'd rather it was only

Harry and not Jessa's entire family changed. Or worse, killed for sport.

"And if you need backup?" Mal made no attempt to hide his irritation. "If Gentry can't get a clean shot?"

"Five minutes." Finn looked him in the eyes. "Five minutes, Mal."

"Got it."

Finn went back down the roof stairs of the shop catty-corner from Jessa's home. She lived in a declining neighborhood of old homes in a forgotten part of the city, far from the growth surrounding the major highways. Far enough off the beaten path that bad things could happen without getting too much attention.

This morning Thomas had shown up on the Talbot doorstep, and Gentry had freaked. Finn knew time was of the essence. He'd like to think Thomas was scouting the place, looking for any sign of Jessa and her whereabouts. But he couldn't leave Harry alone and unprotected. At the same time, Harry had no idea of what was happening in the world around him, and Finn would like to keep it that way.

He knocked on the wooden front door, waving at Harry through the glass oval in its center.

"Mr. Dean?" Harry's surprise was evident. "Finn, I mean."

"Hey, Harry." He shook his hand. "You're here."

"Oh, come on in," he said, looking embarrassed as he stepped back to let him pass. "I got a call about a possible gas leak on the block. They said it was an emergency."

"So you left class and headed home?" The hairs on the back of his neck spiking up. Thomas was here, Finn could smell him.

"I figured 'emergency' meant get over here ASAP," he said, heading down the hall.

Finn followed, trying not to act like he was ready to attack. "And is it an emergency? What's the problem?"

"Don't know. He's checking." Harry nodded at Thomas, who was decked out in what resembled a gas company uniform.

Finn stared, and Thomas stared back at him, the white-knuckled grip on his binder giving him away. Finn grinned, unable to resist the anger and challenge in Thomas's gaze. The boy thought he could fight? Finn would be only too happy to prove him wrong—again—but away from Harry. His skin tightened, wanting to shift.

"I was stopping by to get some things for your sister. I can handle this if you can get these things together?" He handed Harry the bogus list he'd made up. He shook his head, smiling.

"Sure, I'll be back," Harry said, reading over the list. "Make yourself at home."

Thomas stayed in his seat, his arms crossed over his chest, a little too confident for Finn's liking.

"Why are you here?" Finn asked, not moving.

Thomas glanced out the window, the muscle in his jaw working. "Waiting."

"For?" he asked, his gut tightening.

"You," he said, looking at him.

Finn rolled his head, stretching the aching muscles of his neck. His wolf wanted to shift, demanded he shift. "I'm here."

He nodded. "You're here, protecting her brother from me." His anger was barely controlled. "And you have no idea where she is."

Finn's heart stopped, turning frigid. She was safe. With Brown. But the victory in Thomas's eyes had doubt pressing the air from his lungs.

"You haven't heard from her? She didn't make it to Houston."

His skin bristled, the wolf forcing his way out. He pressed his eyes shut, reaching for the medallion that no longer hung about his neck. Jessa had it… Jessa. His fingers popped, the joints dislocating, adjusting for the shift. His arms shook, trembling with restraint. He couldn't lose it now.

"Okay," Harry said, coming into the kitchen. "I have never seen a red sweater, but she had this red sweatshirt so—" He broke off. "Where's the gas company guy?"

Finn's eyes popped open and he pushed off the counter. Where was he? He ran down the hall, slamming out the front door. No Thomas. Finn needed to know the truth. Once he had that, he would enjoy tearing the fucker's throat out.

"Finn?" Harry followed him onto the front porch. "You okay?"

Finn spun, staring at him. "Yeah," he managed, ignoring his rage and pain and fear. "But I need you to do something for me. No questions."

Harry frowned. "I don't work for you, Mr. Dean—"

Finn shook his head, running his hand through his head. "Harry, please don't push me right now."

"What the hell is going on?" Harry asked. "I appreciate you giving my sister a promotion. I do. We need the money. But I'm starting to get a different vibe. What, exactly, are you paying her for? Because, as big and powerful and rich as you are, Jessa's my sister, and it's my job to protect her."

Finn deflated. "I love your sister, Harry. She's everything to me. And protecting her is exactly what I'm trying to do."

Harry blinked, crossing his arms over his chest. "She needs protecting?"

He nodded, glancing at his watch. Where was Mal? Maybe he was tracking Thomas? He could hope. He leaned forward, waving at Gentry. "In a few minutes, an SUV will be here. From now on I need your word that you will not go out alone, no matter what, no questions asked."

"Dude, finals are in a few weeks—"

"I wouldn't ask if it weren't serious, Harry. I'll make sure you don't get penalized for this." He paced the porch, unwilling to leave Harry unprotected. Thomas was messing with him, getting in his head. It was an effective way to torment his enemy.

"You can do that? Just like that?" Harry asked.

"Money can do just about anything, Harry, except keep you safe." He stared at the young man, recognizing the way his forehead furrowed—just like Jessa.

"Safe?" Harry asked.

Finn nodded.

Harry sighed. "Shit."

A car pulled up and Gentry got out. Finn met him on the curb, hoping to keep Harry as clueless as possible.

"Mal tailing him?" Finn asked.

Gentry nodded. "He went out the back window. Mal was almost on him at the corner. I would have taken the shot but Mal was in the way."

Finn swallowed down his frustration. "Take the Talbots to my apartment. Extra security, lock-down until I figure out where to send them." He pulled out his phone. "I need to contact Brown."

Gentry nodded.

Brown's phone rang and rang, ratcheting his unease up to full blown panic. Had he been played, lured from Jessa, leaving her vulnerable? He didn't want to believe it. But his wolf wanted blood.

Chapter Fourteen

Jessa had been in and out of consciousness for some time. The rhythmic spin of the wheels, the low hum of the engine, lulled her back into the dark. But the occasional bump or stop jolted her awake, bracing, waiting for someone to come get her. Then what? Cyrus's words offered some sort of comfort—if he honored them. But being kept prisoner until her baby was born… It was a good thing she was too scared to cry, or she'd have made herself sick.

She tried not to think about Brown. Or her brothers. Or Oscar. Or Finn. She tried to focus on staying calm. She needed to be strong for the baby in her belly. Finn's baby. A wolf, strong and proud, loyal and fierce.

She had no idea how long they'd been driving, only that her left arm was completely numb from being pinned beneath her. Her back stung. Her body throbbed, the bag over her head stuck to her temple, sealing in the heat, sweat, and smell of her own blood.

The car went over several bumps, slowing considerably. She heard voices and a door opening, but the engine was still running. What now?

Cold air. The car door was open. She pushed away, trying to press herself into the other side of the car. But that door opened too and a huge hand encircled her upper arm and tugged her from the car. She stumbled, uncertain in the darkness that still covered her.

"Why did he bring her here?" a voice asked, softly—nervous.

"He wants Dean. But if he can't get him, his offspring is the next best thing," another voice, hard and gruff, answered.

"She's breeding?"

"Shut up, he's coming." The hard voice snapped.

"Look who's up and on her feet?" Cyrus's voice.

She wanted to run, to curl in on herself. But the hand was tugging her forward, uncaring when she tripped or stumbled.

"Any news?" Cyrus asked.

"Thomas is on the run," the other voice answered. He must be the one dragging her along. "The angry one is following him. Thomas is not sure he can outrun him."

"And he's bringing him here?" Cyrus asked.

"I guess so—"

"You guess so?" Cyrus repeated.

They came to an abrupt stop.

"Find out," Cyrus growled, making the hair on the back of her neck stand straight up.

"Yes, sir," the voice said. "What do I do with her?"

There was a long pause. "Take her to Ellen. I want a full work-up before she goes below."

"Yes, sir," the voice repeated.

"And find out about Thomas," Cyrus snapped.

They were moving again, so quickly her feet barely touched the ground. "Stairs, going up," the voice said before pulling her up the steps.

She was out of breath, aching and miserable, when they

stopped again.

"Ellen," the voice said. "Cyrus wants a full work up on her. She's breeding."

"She's breeding?" the woman's voice was incredulous. "Is she one of us?"

"No," Jessa spoke. "I'm not a werewolf."

The bag was snatched off her head, tearing the scab free. Jessa winced, covering the wound on her temple and blinking rapidly from the overwhelmingly bright light.

"You're the mate?" The woman, Ellen, stared at her, circling her slowly.

"Can we get her buckled in?" Jessa stared at the hulk of a man still gripping her arm. "I've got things to do."

Ellen nodded. "Be careful with her, Byron."

Byron snorted, tugging her across the office to what looked suspiciously like an examination table. She resisted then, eyeing the wrist and ankle straps with growing panic. She kicked at him, clawing his forearm to get away. Byron lifted her up and slammed her onto the exam table. "Stop it," he snarled.

"Careful. I know it's a foreign concept to you, but try, Byron. She's important." Ellen patted Jessa. "Very important. I don't think the straps are necessary. Do you?" she asked Jessa.

"Ellen," the man argued. "He'll have a shit-fit if she gets away."

"Where will she go?" Ellen waved her hand at him. "Relax Byron. I swear, I'll have to start treating you for high blood pressure."

Byron scowled at Ellen, but he released Jessa. She rubbed her arm, knowing it would be bruised. And her head throbbed.

"If I have to hear one more fucking word about survival of the pack, live pups, and that goddamn bone, I'm going to challenge him myself," Byron snapped, eyeing Jessa. "I'm not the only one. Some of us think he's bringing a shit-storm of trouble down on us for nothing."

Jessa listened, wishing the words made more sense. Finn had mentioned a bone. The bone that turned him. But the rest of it?

Ellen glanced at the door. "Don't let anyone else hear you say that," she whispered.

Byron stared down at her. He hated her. That was an understatement. His hostility was smothering, pressing in on her until it was hard to breathe.

"Go on," Ellen shooed him from the room. Ellen leaned against the closed door, cocking her head. She smiled at Jessa, her eyes narrowing slightly. "You have no idea what's going on, do you?"

Jessa shook her head.

"Why don't you rest for a bit? We'll see what sort of injuries we're dealing with and go from there." Ellen crossed to her, moving too quickly to put Jessa at ease. "Relax now," Ellen said, patting her thigh.

Jessa frowned, beyond confused.

While Ellen opened and closed cabinets, collecting band aids and alcohol wipes, Jessa was staring wide-eyed at her new surroundings.

It was like any doctor's office. But the charts on the walls differed. Some were human, men and women, others were dogs. No windows, one door, one stool, two chairs, and the examination table she was on—thankfully unsecured.

Ellen sat on the stool and scooted close to Jessa's head. She clicked her tongue, using a cotton ball to clean the sticky mess from her skin and hair. "There's some glass here. Head wounds bleed a lot, so we'll have to see what's going on. Might need stitches. Might be nothing."

Jessa glanced at her. Was Ellen being genuine? Or was she all pretense with big teeth and an even bigger agenda underneath. She had one of those faces that made age irrelevant, lined but lovely in a timeless way. Close-cropped black hair, plain white t-shirt, jeans, and the most unusual eyes. One green and one brown.

"I won't bite," Ellen smiled.

Jessa shook her head.

"I mean, I can. We wolves tend to do that now and then. But I'm civilized," Ellen smiled.

"Why am I here?" Jessa asked.

Ellen glanced at the door. "Besides luring the big one here, you mean? You're pregnant, girl. That's something that hasn't happened in our pack in decades." She paused. "I'm going to wrap your head. I think stitches will do more damage than good."

Jessa frowned.

"I'm not going to bore you with all the details. Let's just say Cyrus doesn't like mysteries." The woman lifted Jessa's hand, peering at the shredded palm. "Ouch. And you—that is, *his* whole pack, the False Wolves—you're all a big, scary mystery to an alpha like Cyrus."

Finn's pack. The False Wolves?

"Glass in here," Ellen said. "I need to get the tweezers. You want anything to eat or drink? Byron's not the most hospitable caretaker."

"Water?" Jessa asked. She was parched. "Please."

Ellen's brow furrowed, her smile tightening. "Sure."

"Ellen," she paused. "Is my baby safe?"

Ellen sat back on her chair, her peculiar gaze settling on Jessa's stomach. "I'd like to say yes, girl. But with Cyrus, there are no guarantees. We'll just have to wait and see." She patted Jessa's thigh again, stood, and stepped out of the room.

Jessa closed her eyes, digging deep for strength. She sat up, pushing off the table and crossing to the door. She opened it slowly, holding her breath as she peered outside. Byron stood across the hall, his arms crossed over the wall of his chest. He cocked one thick eyebrow at her and shook his head. For the first time, she wished Finn hadn't just made her his mate. She wished he'd made her a wolf. Then she'd have a fighting chance.

She didn't see much else before Ellen appeared, walking her back inside the room and closing the door behind them.

"Here ya go," Ellen said, unperturbed by Jessa's curiosity. She offered her a bottle of water. "Need to stay hydrated. Especially considering what you've been through. Finish up and I'll get the glass out of your hands."

Ellen busied herself opening the medical packets she'd brought with her into the room.

Jessa took a sip of the water, praying Ellen's intentions were good. She gulped down the cold water, not realizing just how thirsty she was. But once the bottle was empty, she couldn't keep her eyes open. Water wasn't the only thing in the bottle.

"Shit" Ellen's voice. "Byron! Did you put something in her water? You stupid sonofabitch!"

• • •

Finn stared at the small grocery store, his heart in his throat. He could smell her—faintly. An old scent trail, but it was Jessa. She'd been here.

He choked off his motorcycle and went inside, his eyes sweeping the store. It was late. The clerk was red-eyed, reading a local newspaper. A couple of teenagers were shoving candy in their pants. An old woman was reading the packages of adult diapers.

He grabbed a bottle of water and some gum and headed to the counter.

"Anything else?" the clerk asked.

"I'm looking for them," he said, pulling the photos of Brown and Jessa from his pocket, adding a hundred-dollar bill beneath the pictures.

The clerk eyed the money and tucked it into his pocket, nodding. "Here last night. Cute couple. Probably headed off somewhere to celebrate."

"Celebrate?" Finn asked.

"You don't buy two pregnancy tests if you get a negative the first time around. She was in the bathroom with one. He came up five minutes later to buy another one."

Finn stared at the man, blood roaring in his ears. "These two? You're sure?"

The clerk nodded. "She's prettier than the average three a.m. customers."

Finn nodded, willing his focus onto one thing—finding them. He stared down at the picture of Jessa. "Which way did they go?"

"East, I think." The clerk shrugged.

Finn nodded, pushed through the doors, and climbed onto his bike. His lungs struggled to find air. Jessa was pregnant? He stared at her picture. Harry had given it to him. She was smiling, almost laughing. She was the most beautiful thing in his world. He needed her to come home. To be at his side, with Oscar. And their new baby? His heart constricted tightly, the pain blinding. *Where are you?*

This was his fucking fault. All of it. He'd lost control, given in to his weakness, and now she was pregnant, which was probably why Cyrus took her. He couldn't lose her. He drew in a deep breath, drained the water bottle, and pocketed the gum, all while working through his options. Sitting there doing shit wasn't one of them.

With a final look at the drugstore, he walked into the tall trees behind the building and stripped. He stored his clothes beneath a towering pine, and let his wolf take over. He didn't have time to register pain—the shift was quick—before he was off and running. The wolf didn't give a shit about pain. All it knew was Jessa was missing, gone. And it couldn't deal with that.

Fuck it. *He* couldn't deal. When it came to Jessa, he and the wolf were the same. They needed her like they needed air.

Ten hours. Ten hours with no word, no returned phone calls, no texts, nothing but silence. And he and his wolf were close to losing their shit.

He ran, his paws silent on the fallen needles and damp moss covering the ground. He sifted through the heavy earth, the clean, fresh odor of the forest—dirt, plants, animals. Beyond the green, growing things was the highway. Jessa. He drew her deep into his lungs, tracking her scent along the side of the highway. Around a hundred miles from the drugstore, the scents changed. Metal. Oil. Rubber. Smoke. Flames. Blood. Lots of blood. Metal. Brown. Jessa. Unfamiliar. But they ended. Cut short by the sting of bleach. Someone had covered their scents.

Someone who'd know to cover their scents.

He ran across the road, his nose working overtime now. Jessa had been here. Her scent was strong. Unlike the rest of the ground, the leaves and dirt were displaced—as if someone had fallen. Jessa had fallen. The scent of her blood filled his nostrils and clamped down on his heart. He spun, sifting through the leaves for more. There was a trail, there had to be.

She couldn't just disappear.

He ran onto the road, sniffing the asphalt and gravel, needing answers…

Cars. Lots of traffic. More bleach. Muddying who went where.

His frustration mounted, tearing a howl from his throat as he made the run back to his bike. The run took too long, his impatience and worry making each mile stretch out before him. He pushed, mindless of his bloody paws and aching lungs, until the drugstore was in sight. Tension tightened every muscle and nerve, making his shift painful and his skin itch. His phone was ringing before he'd finished dressing.

"What's going on? Where are you?" Dante asked. "Where's Mal?"

"Tracking Thomas," Finn snapped.

Dante sighed. "And you? I'm not going to sit here on my ass while you two—"

"I need your help," he interrupted. "I think Brown and Jessa were in an accident. Call all the hospitals in the Lake Viking, Missouri area. See if a man and a woman were brought in."

Dante paused. "Lake Viking only?"

He was reeling. "To start."

"Keep it together, man." Dante's voice lowered. "Brown's got her. She'll be okay."

"They bleached the road, Dante. Whoever they are, wherever they went, they knew to cover their tracks." He could barely say the words.

"Shit." Dante said. "We'll find her. Keep your phone handy."

Finn hung up, finished dressing, and headed back to his bike. He plugged in the closest trauma equipped hospital, and roared down the highway. But then a text from Anders had him turning around for a different facility. A reported three-car collision resulting in two fatalities, both men, and two in critical condition—a man and a woman

He broke all speed records as he flew down the highway. She was alive, he had to believe that. That was all he needed to know. She'd be okay, he'd make sure of that.

And Brown? The man was tough, tougher than any other human Finn knew.

And the baby…if there was a baby? The clerk could have

been mistaken. He hoped he was. His dalliance with Cara had been brief, but his son was a gift he loved more every day. He was sorry for Cara's death, but losing Jessa—he couldn't think about it.

Hollis was still trying to determine the cause of Cara's death. Which meant it could have been a car accident. Or it could have resulted from delivering Oscar. If it was the latter, he would do everything in his power to stop something from happening to Jessa.

First things first, he had to get to her. To touch her and tell her he loved her.

"I'm Finnegan Dean," he said to the med tech at the reception desk.

"Oh." The woman jumped up, nervous. "Dr. Robbins called. Follow me."

"What rooms?" he snapped. She'd only slow him down.

"A210 and A211, but—"

Finn took the stairs, sprinting to the second floor and pushing through the door. He scanned the sign on the wall, read the room numbers, and turned left. Most of the overhead lights were dimmed—it was three in the morning.

When he reached A211, he slipped inside and stared at the bed. In it was an unfamiliar woman, unconscious and hooked up to wires.

He hurried to A210 and recognized Brown. The man's eyes were shut, his face a patchwork of angry colors. His heart rate was strong and even.

"Brown?" he murmured.

Brown's eyes popped open, blinking frantically.

"Where is Jessa?" Finn asked, desperate for answers.

The man's eyes fell shut, his nostrils flaring. He sucked in a shuddering breath. "Cyrus—"

"Where is she?" his voice grew rough, menacing.

Brown's eyes met his. "He killed her."

Finn shook his head. "No."

"I saw it." Brown's nod was jerky. "Saw her."

Finn glared at the man. "Saw it?" His voice rose. "But didn't stop it?"

"I'm sorry. I couldn't." Brown's voice broke.

Finn wasn't listening. His wolf wanted to take its frustrations out on Brown—the last person with her. His wolf needed an outlet, someone to blame. And Brown was there, apologizing for letting Jessa go. But deep down, Finn knew Brown couldn't have stopped Cyrus. His bodyguard was a human. Protecting Jessa was Finn's responsibility. He had failed her. "She wasn't there. Are you sure?" Why would Cyrus have taken her body? Why not leave her there, proof of the damage he'd done. An invisible noose seemed to tighten around his throat.

Brown nodded.

If she were dead, he would know. He'd feel it. Wouldn't he? Blood roared in his ears, rejecting Brown's words. This was wrong.

But the smell of her blood. Too much. He swallowed, leaning forward to brace himself against the side of the bed. Better to hold on to the anger. Anger, he could work with. Fury, he could handle.

"Finn, he's baiting you." Brown's voice was stronger. "He wants to bring you to your knees. This is about control—"

"Control?" Finn stared at the man. His wolf raged to get out, crumbling Finn's defenses. Jessa was gone. Cyrus had taken her. And Finn would make him pay for it.

Chapter Fifteen

Jessa sat on the cot against the wall. Her legs were drawn up and hugged tightly to her chest, her cheek pressed to her knees.

"Still hurting?" Ellen asked, carrying in a tray with food.

Jessa nodded.

"I brought soup and crackers." Ellen placed the tray on the small table against the far side of the room. "Come on, Jessa, you need to eat something. The baby needs you to eat something."

Jessa frowned at her. Ellen denied having a hand in drugging her, but Jessa didn't know who to trust. She'd fallen asleep in her own clothes and woken up in a hospital gown with an IV in her arm. She'd promptly ripped the needle out and stayed huddled in the corner of the stone room for however long she'd been there.

The place was small. A bed, table, and chair. No clock. But someone had provided a dog-eared copy of a baby name book.

"Yes, eat." Cyrus followed Ellen inside. "Leave," he said

to Ellen, never looking her way. He turned the chair backward and straddled it, resting his hands and chin on the top. His pale gaze pinned her, unblinking and unwavering.

Jessa wasn't aware of Ellen leaving, only that they were alone, and the room felt incredibly small and cold.

She shivered.

"You're cold?" he asked, unmoving.

She shook her head.

"You're frightened of me." He smiled, one eyebrow arching.

Her heart was racing.

"You are appealing, Jessa Talbot. Weak, vulnerable, and soft. If you weren't his…" He let the words hang there. "But you are. Not just his plaything, but his mate. A human." He chuckled. "A strong human. Your scar, his mark, looks painful."

A shiver slid over her. He'd seen her scars? He'd seen her bare skin? Her hands smoothed the hospital gown down. She didn't feel very strong.

"Talk to me," he said, his voice deceptively soft. But Jessa heard the demand.

"What do you want me to say?" she whispered, avoiding his gaze.

"I want to know about his pack. How many are there? Where are they? Sharing such information will prevent things from getting unpleasant." He paused. "We call them the False Wolves. Did you know that?"

She shook her head, considering all the ways "unpleasant" could be translated.

"They shouldn't exist." He ran his finger across his lower lip, his attention wandering to her mouth. "Do you believe in accidents, Miss Talbot? Or are you one who subscribes to a higher plan? Destiny. Fate. That sort of thing?"

"I'm not sure." Her answer was soft, uncertain.

"I am the latter. You live as long as I have, and you see it plainly enough. Accidents don't exist. And Mr. Dean's *transformation* means something. Do you know what it means?" he asked, leaning forward.

She shook her head, fighting the urge to recoil.

"It's a test. To see who's stronger. Who's meant to survive and rule." He sat back, shrugging. "It's my job to adapt. I've had years of practice, Miss Talbot. Years and years. Your mate is a pup in comparison. A pup I will annihilate."

"What about the bone?" she asked, remembering Hollis's theory. The bone might threaten Cyrus's place as alpha—and his pack. Did it make Finn their leader? She broke off, watching Cyrus's eyes narrow, his lips press tight.

"What about it, Miss Talbot?" He stood, pushing the chair in.

She stared up at him, terrified.

"Please, continue." He paused, his hands clasped behind his back. "And spare no detail, I implore you."

Cyrus had to suspect something, or he'd have killed Finn by now—or tried to. At this point, there was nothing left for her to lose. He would kill her. He'd told her as much. She had no experience with head games or manipulating emotions, but she'd try. Her future wasn't looking too bright, but that didn't have to apply to the rest of her pack.

"It's old," she said, meeting his gaze. "Older than you."

Cyrus's nostrils flared.

"It's what turned Finn, infected him. Doesn't that make him your ancestor?" Her voice was quavering, but there was no help for that. She pushed on, watching him carefully. "Killing him risks your life, right? And your status as alpha to your pack?"

He stared at her, the muscle in his jaw ticking.

"Is that what you mean?"

He smiled at her. "Your loyalty is admirable, truly. But tell me, Miss Talbot, what will you do when he's tired of you? No wolf stays bonded to a human. It's not a true bond unless it's with another wolf. Didn't he tell you?" He paused, his mock sympathy cutting deep. "You'll go on loving him while he moves on to one of his own kind."

She swallowed, refusing to believe him. Finn loved her—he'd chosen her. He was the one that warned her he'd never let her go. Her hand fell to her stomach, covering the scar. And now, their baby. "He is mine. And I am his."

Cyrus chuckled, surprised. "You believe that?"

She nodded. "I know it."

"Has he offered to turn you?" he asked. He waited, almost eagerly, for her response.

She kept her silence. They'd never discussed it.

"No? That's unfortunate, isn't it? Considering you won't survive this pregnancy. No human has," he said. "Cara didn't, poor thing. I'm sorry Miss Talbot." He eyed her stomach. "Perhaps there's no point in waiting? Perhaps he's already moved on. He has one pup, already. I can't imagine he's eager for another one so soon."

She couldn't speak, couldn't trust her words not to reveal her agitation. A reaction she knew he'd enjoy.

"I'll have to think about that," he said, opening the door. "For now, there's someone who'd like to see you."

Thomas stepped inside, his nervous gaze darting between Jessa and Cyrus.

"Do not touch her," Cyrus commanded before he left, the door remaining slightly ajar.

"What do you want?" she whispered, tears welling up in her eyes. "What did you do to my brother?"

He scowled at her.

"How could you Thomas? I thought we were friends?" She covered her face, too tired and fraught to care anymore.

"We were friends. Are friends. Harry's fine. Nice kid." He

paused. "I needed to buy some time to get you here. Safe."

She looked at him. "Safe?" She lifted her hair to show him the gash on her forehead. Then held her hands up, palms out, for his inspection. "You handed me over to them."

Thomas knelt by the edge of the bed. "Who's to say Finn's on the right side of things, Jessa? I know you like him—that he's in your head—but you need to think through this. Listen to me."

She held her hand up. "No."

Thomas reached for but stopped short. Cyrus's command. Even without the alpha in the room, Thomas obeyed. "Because you're scared. I get it. I was scared too. But there are things you need to know. This baby will kill you."

She leaned away from him. "Cyrus says."

"And Ellen." He stood, shaking his head. "Ask her to see his pet's medical files, the one that birthed his first child. Ask her what happened. Finn's doc knows too. He has the same file. He's just not telling you because he wants to grow his pack."

"And you, Thomas?" she asked. "What excuse did Cyrus use to justify turning you?"

Thomas frowned. "I wanted to be turned, Jessa. I asked for this. And it's a good damn thing, too. Because now I can stop you from making the wrong decision. You're where you belong now, with me."

• • •

"It's fucking freezing," Gentry said, chewing on his unlit cigar. "Where the fuck are we? And what is that smell?"

"The middle of nowhere Nebraska." Dante muttered. "I can't feel my toes."

Finn's patience was slipping away. He didn't want them here. He'd left, fully intending to vent his fury—the wolf's fury—on the Others himself. But they'd followed him, spouting crap about being a pack, looking out for one another, and family. He'd wanted to jump Dante when he mentioned Oscar. He didn't need reminding that his son was alone, that he needed his father to come back in whole and unharmed.

But Finn wasn't whole anymore. The last three days, a gaping hole had eaten its way through his heart. He felt it, held on to it, to keep him going. He'd lost his soulmate. She was gone. He winced, the air escaping his lungs on a razor's edge.

Oscar would be better off without him.

They all would. If he killed Cyrus, they'd all be free. He didn't care about frostbitten toes and the smell of rotting hay. All he cared about, all he could think about, was ripping Cyrus's throat out and watching every drop of blood seep into the dirt.

He'd imagined it over and over—calming his wolf when his control wavered. It gave them focus and purpose. He would do this, one way or the other. He just hoped like hell that Mal, Dante, and Gentry didn't fuck things up.

"Cornfields as far as the eye can see," Gentry said. "Good cover for a pack of wolves."

"No way this is his only hangout," Mal interrupted. "There are too many of them to all hole-up here."

Finn agreed. He hoped like hell Cyrus was here, if nothing else, he'd take down Thomas—Mal had followed the piece of shit here. And, for now, it was the only lead he had. Once his wolf got a hold of Thomas, he'd find out where Cyrus was.

Trying to sneak up on a place with no variations in the terrain was a challenge for a group. Another reason he'd wanted to come alone. They'd wasted time on some half-assed plan, shifting back and forth, and covering their tracks.

"Two ways to get in," Mal had said, pointing at the computer screen and Google map image on the drive there.

"Main drive and the dirt road for the farm equipment."

"How many?" Finn asked, talking into his earpiece at Anders—monitoring the place via satellite on his computer and relaying everything directly into Finn's ear.

"Infrared is only picking up heat in part of the rooms," Anders said. "Meaning some of them are lined. You sure you want to do this?"

He almost growled in frustration. "How many?" he repeated.

"Twenty-two," Anders said.

"How many?" Mal asked.

"Twenty-five," Finn said. "Maybe more."

Mal grinned, slapping Dante on the shoulder. "Sounds like we're all gonna get some action today."

Dante nodded. He lacked Mal and Gentry's enthusiasm, but he'd refused to stay behind.

"News on Brown?" Gentry asked, sloshing forward through the icy water.

"He and the girl are at the safe house. Hollis has her under lock-down, just in case she wakes up with an ax to grind." Anders asked, "She really Brown's daughter?"

"We'll know when they wake up," Mal said.

It had taken everything he had not to wake her up. He wanted to shake her until she told him what he needed to know. What were Cyrus's weaknesses? How could Finn hurt him most?

"Finn?" Anders spoke into the ear piece. "No distractions. Jessa's brothers are safe here, all googly-eyed over Oscar. We're good." Anders sighed. "I know you're pissed man, but don't lose your head. Jessa—"

Finn pulled out his earpiece. He couldn't hear her name, it set the wolf off—made him crazed. Not yet. Not yet.

"It's time," Finn said.

Gentry was wearing his hell-yes smile, toting every

firearm known to man.

"I'm ready," Mal said, bouncing on the ball of his feet.

Finn shook his head. It was a shit plan, but the only one they had. "Be careful," he said, clasping Mal's hand in his.

Mal shook his head. "Can't promise that."

"We'll bring the cavalry," Gentry said, still grinning.

Mal waved and left, sprinting up onto the highway and across, into the corn-field that surrounded Cyrus's farm. In five-minutes, he'd cause a diversion, then they'd go in.

"Nothing like freezing your ass off in an ice bath to make you remember the good old days," Gentry said, laughing. "Hunting the bad guys, tromping through hellacious terrain, and—my favorite—blowing shit up."

Finn focused on the horizon. Mal's signal, courtesy of Gentry's skill with plastic explosives, should rock the ground under their feet and light up the sky. And it would stop all their pointless conversations. The wolf was done with pretending to be human. Finn's eyes narrowed, anticipation rippling down his spine. The urge to shift was undeniable.

"Anytime now," Dante said, glancing at his watch.

A few seconds later, the sky exploded. Orange, yellow, red, and white streaked up into the early morning sky.

"I'd say that'll get their attention." Dante grinned, clapping Gentry on the back.

"Damn straight," Gentry agreed. "Giving you five minutes, starting now."

Finn shifted, giving his wolf what he wanted: ultimate control. He'd never felt the surge of the hunt so clearly. Never wanted to see what his wolf was capable of. Now, he couldn't wait to get started.

"Holy shit," Gentry said. "Gets me every time." He smiled at Finn. "See you in there, boss."

Finn took off, his paws tearing up the ground as his nose led the way. Dante was at his side, letting him lead but staying close. They skirted the field, staying in the shadows, until the house was in sight. It looked like something out of *The Walton's*. Big and white, a traditional farmhouse. Full of traditional werewolves. More Stephen King than *Little House on the Prairie*.

Despite the light show, there was not a sound. No sign of a wolf.

The fur on his shoulders pricked straight up.

Where the hell was everyone?

The barn was blazing, flames leaping high enough to ignite the dry stalks. It was only a matter of time before the fields went up and the fire spread to the house and outbuildings. Yet no one was attempting to put the flames out. It was still. Silent. They knew they were coming.

Dante nudged his haunch before sprinting off. He'd loop around and bring up the rear.

Finn's wolf snapped his teeth, his adrenaline thumping through his veins and making his blood roar. He made a full circle around the house, slipping out of the corn when the stalks began to burn. Heat wafted up, smoke stinging his nose, and making his eyes water. Each slip of husk on husk, each snap of a dry stem beneath his paws, echoed in his ears. The crackle and pop of the fire helped cover his movements somewhat. But his nerves were on edge, amplifying everything. He might as well wear a fucking cowbell or light-up collar.

A scent reached him, faint, buried beneath the smoke. It teased him, a flare of recognition, then nothing but singed corn and scorched earth.

He put his nose down, jogging away from the flaming crops. A new scent. Blood. He froze, his chest heavy and thick. Mal's blood.

He hesitated, then stepped forward, staring through the corn at the neatly mowed lawn. There was one tree with sprawling branches and a spare canopy of dry, withered leaves. And hanging from one thick limb was Mal. The wolf hung upside down, his throat torn open. Blood dripping. A rhythmic tap… His blood forming a puddle, soaking the ground.

No. This was Cyrus's fate. Cyrus. Not Mal. His throat tightened, needing to howl, needing to call out. Mal. Goddammit Mal.

Finn ran forward, blood roaring in his veins and vision gone red.

The Others were on him then. A swarm of teeth and fur and claws. They tried to stop him, to get in his way, but they didn't last long. A bite to the neck was fastest. But crunching through the nose worked. It was surprisingly easy to break a back. And slit the skin of a belly.

He never slowed.

Not until Mal was down, laying on the blood-soaked ground at his feet. He nudged him, sniffing Mal's limp body.

"He's not going to make it." Cyrus's voice reached him. "It seems you have a problem protecting your pack, Mr. Dean."

Finn spun, choking on bile and hate.

Cyrus stood on the porch, leaning against the pillar. His pale gaze locked with his. "While I have lost no one," he taunted, tempting the wolf. "You've lost…two? Or three? Considering she was carrying your pup."

Finn paced back and forth, a low growl resonating in his throat.

"Now my farm," Cyrus said. "It's a total loss." His eyes narrowed. "Have you come here to kill me, Finn? For vengeance? Or are you planning on torturing me first? Nothing you do will ease the pain. Nothing." He smiled.

Finn heard Dante howl in the distance. He was on his own, he had to keep it together.

His wolf would not be calmed. His vision was bright red, his ears seeking the wet slosh of Cyrus's accelerated heart rate. He wanted to stop that sound, wanted to rip the beating organ from his chest and devour it. He growled, pacing back and forth.

"So angry," Cyrus said, watching. "Out of control. How unlike you, Finn." Cyrus's gaze wandered beyond him, a slight crease forming behind his brows as he took in the carnage.

"Let me fight him," Thomas stepped forward, breathing heavy.

"You think you can best him, Thomas? Fight him," Cyrus said. "I'm not stopping you."

Finn shook his head and regarded Thomas. The boy wouldn't stand a chance. *Don't.*

Thomas smiled. "Scared, playboy?"

Finn shook his head again, his wolf snapping in anticipation. *Don't.* He glanced at Cyrus, saw the fascination in his pale eyes, and gritted his teeth. He wanted them to fight, wanted to watch. And it sickened Finn.

But Thomas was turning.

And Finn's wolf—his thirst for the kill—took over. He waited for Thomas to finish. And once Thomas's wolf was done, Finn smelled his fear. He was smaller. So were the others he'd fought. They'd been small, weaker, and slower.

He circled Thomas, ignoring the snap and growl of the wolves waiting for their turn. They respected the challenge, but for how long?

Thomas stepped forward. Finn bit into his foreleg, pulling it out from under him and flipping the wolf over. But Finn let go and stepped back, letting Thomas rise. Thomas growled, planting his forelegs and posturing, even as he shifted his weight from his wounded leg.

Finn snorted, shaking his head.

Thomas charged, eyes wild and mouth open. But Finn side-stepped, his jaws latching on to Thomas's throat, snapping hard, before flinging him up and over. Thomas's body slammed into the ground with all his force, the sickening crunch of bone signaling Finn's victory.

Thomas lay, each breath a strangled groan.

The stillness of the yard made the growing fire that much more obvious. The morning sky was grey, thick with smoke. Flames rose and billowed, sweeping across the vast cornfield and creeping up on the house. Soon the local fire department would come or a neighbor would call this in. And Finn would run out of time.

He stiffened, planting his front feet on the earth. He stuck his chest out, his ears and eyes focusing only on the man that stood before him. His growl turned into a guttural howl, hungry for a fight. There was no mistaking his challenge.

"You have a choice to make," Cyrus said. "Fight me and die." His voice wavered, his gaze once more returning to the carnage Finn had left in his madness. "Or save Jessa."

Finn's heart throbbed to life.

"She's there," Cyrus said, pointing to the small shed at the edge of the yard. The roof was beginning to smoke. "It might already be too late."

It was a trick. Where the fuck was Dante? Finn's jaws snapped in agitation. It was a trick. Brown saw her die.

Cyrus smiled, but it was unsteady. His gaze bounced again and again to his wounded and dead. Did he know that Finn would kill him? That this was where he'd die? Is that why he was taunting Finn? "I tried to convince her your affections weren't true. But she wouldn't believe me. She said you belonged to her. And she belonged to you. She believed that, Finn. Her loyalty is—was," he paused, nodding at the shed, "truly admirable. I was going to keep her until the pup was born, study what happened. I think she's stronger than most humans, but not strong enough to live through birthing your offspring." He shook his head again. There was a desperation to his tone. Cyrus was afraid. "Or, a fire."

Finn wanted Cyrus to fear him. But more than that, he wanted Jessa back.

The sound of fighting was unmistakable. Dante's whimper, the snarl and growl of wolves. Dante couldn't help him. Finn had a choice to make.

Finn's wolf acted. His fury and anger and rage were replaced with the slightest flicker of hope. His paws tore across the yard. He knew Cyrus had used Jessa as a ploy, a way to escape. But he would never be able to live with himself if he was wrong. If she was here. If she was alive.

Dante was with him, then, the pack on their heels.

Gentry fired his big gun then. And the Others were mowed down, or running. He didn't look back.

He circled the building.

A woman, her short black hair bloodied, lay outside the building and blocked the door. Piles of compost surrounded the building, evidence of the packs kills—both human and animal—singed his nose. But it did the job, covering other scents.

The roof was caving in, the flame and heat building as Finn nudged the woman away and to tear at the wood with his teeth. Dante helped and, between the two of them, they ripped the door free of its hinges.

Jessa.

Her scent reached him instantly.

He peered inside, searching through the feed sacks, hay, and shadows. She lay on her side, tied to a chair, unmoving. Of course, it was a trick. Cyrus wouldn't have given her back alive. But her heart was beating. Her pulse was strong and steady. He swallowed, letting the sound of it, the feel of it roll over him. His relief drained his lungs, soothing him and the wolf. And terrifying them.

If the fire hadn't put her in immediate danger, he would have dropped to his knees and cried like a fucking baby. But not now. Pieces of the ceiling fell, a rain of flaming shingles and wood.

Finn shifted instantly, his wolf relinquishing control so they could get her to safety. He knelt by her, his hands gentle on her upper arm.

She screamed, the sound muffled by the gag tied around her mouth. The sound was ragged, exhausted, but she jerked free, fighting the knots that kept her tied to the heavy wooden kitchen chair. She began coughing, wheezing.

"Jessa," his voice broke. She was battered, dried blood and bruises covering far too much exposed skin. But she wasn't listening, she was leaning away from him, her eyes pressed tightly shut. "Jessa?" he said again, more firmly.

"Please." She was hoarse, a fit of coughing reminding him of the precarious position they were in. "Stop."

He tore through the ropes and gently, oh-so-carefully, held her close. The comfort of her weight, the feel of her in his arms, erased every fear. Nothing more would happen to her. He'd make sure of it. "It's me, Jessa. It's Finn." He buried his nose in the hair against her temple as he carried her from the building, cradled against his chest. "I've got you. You're safe."

Chapter Sixteen

Jessa blinked, every breath making her throat spasm and forcing a hacking cough. It had been worse with that filthy rag shoved into her throat. Worse when she'd fallen over, unable to loosen the knotted ropes. Worse when her eyes stung and burned so much she could no longer open them. But now her mind was playing tricks on her.

"Jessa." His voice.

His scent.

She stopped pushing against the wall of muscles that gently held her. Finn? She blinked, wiping her eyes, wincing against the chafing of her lids. The smoke and heat had singed her throat, nose, and eyes to sandpaper.

But she had to see him.

She tried, but the sky was so bright, blinding her. "Finn?" she asked, her throat raw. The air felt lighter now, cleaner, but it still hurt to breathe. And she couldn't stop coughing.

"I'm here, Jessa." He pressed a hard kiss against her temple. "I've got you, you hear me?"

She nodded, relaxing against him. "Finn."

"Shh, it's okay. Dante, she needs water," Finn said, sounding desperate. "Slow breaths, Jessa."

She nodded, twining her arms around his neck and burying her face against his chest. "Wait. Wait, Finn," she said, forcing her eyes open. "Ellen?"

"Ellen?" Dante appeared, a water bottle in his hand.

"She stopped them," Jessa said, wiping at her eyes. They were still watering, preventing her from seeing clearly. "She saved me."

"She saved you?" Finn repeated, his expression fierce.

"Short black hair? Tattoos?" Dante asked, surprising Jessa with his detail.

"Is she…" Jessa's heart sank, her obscured vision catching snippets of smoke, the burning field, and signs of a gruesome fight.

"She's unconscious," Dante assured her.

"Bring her." She sipped the water bottle, the burn making her groan. Finn's hands tightened on her. "Please, bring Ellen. She betrayed them—for me and the baby." She blinked slowly, until she could focus. And all she could see was Finn. "Please."

"Bring her," Finn said, unable to look away from her. He was beautiful. Real. Here. But she'd never seen that expression on his face before. And it scared her.

"Finn?" she asked.

He shook his head, pressing a kiss to her lips. "You're here. You are—" he broke off, clearing his throat roughly. "I'm so sorry Jessa. This should never have happened."

"Finn?" She coughed, her throat too shredded to talk. She sipped the water bottle, her arm wavering. Now was not the time to be weak. She pushed against him. "Walk," she said.

He shook his head. "You might be able to walk. But I'm not ready to let you go." Fear and desperation colored every syllable.

Dante appeared, Ellen's arm draped around his shoulder.

"Car," Ellen said. "Here." She shoved keys at Finn, wheezing heavily. "Go."

"We're going." Jessa agreed worried about the amount of blood Ellen was losing. "And you're coming too."

"Leave me," Ellen argued.

"Shush," Jessa said, slipping from Finn's hold and securing Ellen's other arm around her shoulders. She could feel Finn's disapproval but ignored him.

Ellen was bleeding heavily, but she tried to walk. "Need to shift," she said.

"You'll heal faster?" Jessa remembered Finn saying as much. "Can you?"

Ellen nodded, releasing her.

It looked incredibly painful. With Finn, it had been quick, almost natural. But Ellen's broken and battered state seemed to impede the process. She glanced behind her, expecting Cyrus or Byron to come back — to drag her away. But Finn was here. And he would protect her.

Even now, he put himself behind her, his hands resting on her shoulders.

Where was Cyrus? A knot of apprehension rose in her chest, pressing against her ribs. It was still hard to breathe, after inhaling so much smoke. Her tension didn't help. She glanced back, shivering, but there was no sign of Cyrus. Only the billowing black smoke and roaring flames.

Finn's hands squeezed her shoulders. "He's gone, Jessa."

She nodded, stepping closer to him. Finn wouldn't let anything happen to her.

Ellen's wolf sagged, panting heavily. Jessa stood at her side, helping her stay upright as they moved around the house to the truck parked in back. Dante helped Ellen into the truck bed, then said, "I'll help Gentry set the charges," before closing the passenger door and nodding at her.

Jessa smiled as Finn's hand clasped hers. She closed her

eyes, drawing slow breaths. The worst was over. She was safe. They were safe. She opened her eyes as the truck rolled to a stop—and she stared in horror.

The flames were moving quickly, eating up the grass and shrubs that ran the length of the house. But what drew her attention, what she couldn't look away from. Bodies. Not wolves. Men and women—or what was left of them. She pushed open the passenger door and vomited violently. Her head was spinning, her heart racing, and her stomach. She placed a hand against her stomach.

"You okay?" Finn's voice.

She stared at him, seeing the blood and grime that covered his naked body for the first time. She nodded, shock finally kicking in. "I will be," her voice was soft. "How long have I been gone? And my family? Oscar?"

"Three days." His hand tightened around hers. "Everyone's safe. Everyone wants you home." His gaze falling to her stomach.

She loved the look on his face. She was his, irrefutably. Cyrus's words were an empty threat, one meant to make her doubt this man—her mate. No, she wasn't a wolf but their bond was sealed by the mark on her body. She trusted him. She reached for him, needing his touch. His fingers laced with hers as he slid into the truck beside her. He pressed a kiss to her temple, breathing her deep.

"Place is gonna blow. How about we cut this reunion short and get the fuck out of here?" Gentry asked, sliding into the truck. Dante tapped the back window, giving the thumbs up sign.

Finn nodded and threw the truck in gear.

His strength seeped into her. She sank against his side. His hand clasped hers, the press of his thigh against hers easing the terror of the last hour, somewhat. But she'd never forget. Never. Mal. She swallowed, not wanting to think about what they'd done to him. He'd come to save her. And died because of it. How could she live with that?

"Who's the wolf?" Gentry asked.

"Ellen. Her name is Ellen," Jessa said. "She's a good guy." At least, that's what Jessa wanted to believe. She wasn't sure what had motivated Ellen's actions but, she didn't care. They wanted to same thing: Jessa and her baby to live. And that was enough.

"You okay?" Gentry asked. "You're lookin' a little pale."

She nodded again. "Rough couple of days."

"Ain't that the truth?" Gentry laughed the sort of laugh that bordered on unstable.

She understood. The morning was a surreal nightmare. But the sounds, smells, images, were vividly etched into her brain. Her hands covered his, desperate for his touch.

"You're cold." Finn was worried.

She nodded, shivering in earnest. "Shock," she managed, unable to stop the chatter of her teeth.

A deafening explosion shook the ground as the corn-field and house turned into a raging inferno.

"Should take care of it," Gentry said, staring out the rear window at his handiwork. "Fire. Propane tanks blow. Unfortunate accident all around."

Jessa looked at the rearview window, the profile of two large wolves sitting, ears perked and staring at the flames, an oddly comforting view. She drew in a deep, unsteady breath, and lay her head back on the seat.

Finn reached across, pulling her closer so her head could fall onto his shoulder. His hand was shaking against her thigh, his breath harsh against her temple. And Jessa couldn't breathe. Her relief was so overwhelming, it choked her. Now was not the time to fall apart, but hot tears filled her eyes.

The shrill phone chirp made them all jump.

"Gentry here," he answered the phone. "No, no, plans

changed." He sighed. "Mr. Dean," he said, handing Finn the phone.

"Yes?" One word, exhausted on every level. "Jessa's alive. We lost Mal."

The silence of the truck cab thickened, forcing tears onto her cheeks.

"Tomorrow." He paused. "We need sleep." He broke off. "I need time alone with Jessa."

They drove on for more than an hour, the mid-morning sun weak in the winter sky. "Smells like snow," Finn said as they pulled into a small town off the highway.

Gentry tossed Finn a bag. "I'll get some rooms."

"I don't want her left alone," Finn said, nodding at Ellen in the truck bed.

Jessa looked at Finn.

"I know she helped you, but I don't trust her." His blue eyes searched hers. "Not yet."

Jessa nodded. She understood. Ellen was unknown. She'd helped Jessa but that didn't mean she'd do the same for the rest of them.

"Got it," Gentry said, patting the truck bed as he went.

Jessa looked back to see Dante wrapped up in a blanket, exhausted. Ellen was still in wolf form, her breathing irregular. "Will she be okay?" Jessa asked.

Finn slid on some sweat pants and shrugged into a t-shirt. "She was smart to shift. She'll heal faster that way. Unless there was too much damage." He shoved the bag out the back window to Dante. "Here," he said.

Finn carried Ellen, covered with a large blanket, through the back doors of the hotel. Jessa followed, unsteady on her feet. The deserted halls and lack of staff told her the hotel was being paid for their anonymity. But after the constant upheaval of the last few days, it seemed too quiet. Finn lay Ellen on a bed in the suite she'd share with Dante and Gentry.

The men's unspoken conversation, awkward, tight hugs and silent thank-you's, was subdued. They'd lost a brother tonight. While her family was safe and sound, unaware of the brutality they'd shared.

"Jessa?" Finn's hand was warm around hers. "Let's get some sleep."

She twined her fingers with his, letting him lead her from the room, down the hall, and into their room. The curtains were pulled tight, keeping out the bright white of the winter day—and the world.

"Shower," Finn said, locking the door.

She stared at the door. The latch. The deadbolt. They seemed so useless, almost comical. Her giggle was involuntary.

He paused, glancing at the door, then her. "I'm sorry, Jessa," his voice wavered.

She shook her head. "You can't be sorry. That implies some sort of regret. And you can't regret this. Us." It was hard to get the words out, but she had to. "You chose me."

"I do," he interrupted, tilting her head back. "Always. Pain is what I regret. Fear."

She stared up at him. "Cyrus tried to convince me that, since I'm not a wolf, this," she paused, placing a hand on his chest, "wasn't real. That if you were serious you'd turn me. But all I could think about was you. I didn't want you hurt. Or your brothers. Your pain is mine. All the fear and pain." She shook her head. "You make up for it, Finn. As long as I have you, I'm good."

He crushed her in his arms, then immediately released her. "I don't know what hurts."

"I'm too happy to hurt, Finn," she admitted. "Shower?" she managed, hoping she could wash away some of the night.

He nodded, leading her into the bathroom.

• • •

It took everything Finn had to keep his temper in check. Her hands. Her forehead. Bruises along her side and hip, scratches. She was a rainbow of angry, sore colors that made his jaw clench with fury. But her cuts and bruises would heal.

Worse, Cyrus had tried to plant doubt about his feelings for her. She'd been alone, afraid, hurting—the perfect time to get into her head. To make her second-guess something she trusted. He hoped she trusted it, them. Hoped she knew he'd meant forever, no matter what.

He couldn't stop touching her.

After thinking she was dead—fear was too fresh, too all-consuming.

He needed reassurance, his wolf needed it. She was here. Close. Even now, his hand rested lightly on the base of her spine as they showered. He watched her, mesmerized by the slide and caress of water against her body. She was beautiful. She stood beneath the water, eyes shut, washing her face. So, damn beautiful.

His.

The wolf wanted to drag her into bed and curl around her. It would take time to ease the panic her abduction had caused. Time his wolf wanted to spend wrapped up in oeach other. Finn agreed.

He lathered himself up over and over, washing away the grit and blood, the fight and anger, of the early morning. He didn't want to think about Cyrus or the Others.

"Done?" he asked, her slight nod enough to make him turn off the water.

He stepped out of the shower, wrapping her in a thick white towel and patting her dry. Her blonde hair fell in heavy locks over her shoulders. Her left shoulder was badly bruised, so he bent, trailing his nose over the contusion and pressing a soft kiss on her skin.

There was a scratch on her neck. He stooped, nuzzling the

skin, drawing her scent deep, and kissed her. He could feel the flutter of her pulse beneath his lips. Steady, slightly elevated. But most importantly, beating and alive.

He cradled her close, sighing at the feel of her against him. "Sleep?" he asked.

"Yes, please," she agreed, wrapping her arms around him.

For a moment, they didn't move. But he knew she needed rest. For herself and the baby. He swung her up in his arms.

"Finn–" her protest was thick, sleepy.

"Hush," he whispered against the top of her head.

Jessa's smell. How he loved her scent, the feel of her in his arms, the sigh she made as she relaxed in his hold. The bed was big, crisp sheets, comfy blankets, and Jessa. He didn't need much more.

Jessa's sleep was fitful, jarring him awake over and over. He reached out for her, wrapping her up in his arms. She tossed, pushing away from him and huddling in a ball. She bolted upright, her hands fisting in the sheets, gasping for breath.

He sat up, running his hand down her back and through her still-damp hair. She'd been through hell. And until she faced it, she'd never be free. "What is it?" he whispered. "Tell me."

She shook her head.

"Jessa," he encouraged her to face him. "You have to let me in."

She stayed stiff, rigid.

He stretched, turning on the bedside light. But seeing her like this, so full of fear, choked him. Her wide green eyes fixed on his face, searching his eyes. Was she afraid of him?

"I'd never hurt you," he vowed.

She nodded.

"I'll protect you, no matter what." He touched her cheek.

She relaxed against him.

"Tell me, so I can make it better," his voice was low.

"It will hurt," she said.

He nodded, bracing himself. What had they done to her?

"M-Mal." She shook her head.

Finn's heart stopped. He placed a hand on her back, needing contact.

"Cyrus brought me out of the cellar—where I'd been staying—so I could see what they were doing to M-Mal," her voice broke. "He was in so much pain. They kept asking him questions, about you, your pack, the bone. He wouldn't say anything."

Finn didn't want to imagine it, but her words left him no choice. Mal, suffering, for him—again.

"They hit me then and he shifted. Cyrus said horrible things, threatened me and Mal fought but th-they cut his throat. He kept bleeding. He told me not to believe them." She buried her face in her hands. "I couldn't do anything, Finn. I couldn't stop the horrible things coming from Cyrus's mouth. Or the injuries they inflicted on Mal. I had to sit there and watch. He kept telling me to be strong. He was alive when they dragged him outside." She stared at him. "I can't stop seeing it. Hearing it."

He'd never been much of a crier. Even when he was young, he'd shrug things off, channeling his emotion into anger or attitude. He ached to cry for Mal, for her, with her.

"You shouldn't have been there, Jessa. I let you down." The weight of failure settled on him. "I didn't do what I promised. I didn't protect you or my pack."

Her arms slid around his neck, soft as silk. "I don't blame you. Mal didn't blame you. He told Cyrus that you'd never stop until he was dead." Her breath wavered. "But after seeing that… I can't lose you. In my dream, it was you, not Mal."

He lifted her hand, pressing a kiss to the tip of every finger. "Hey, hey, I'm here. That will never happen. You need sleep, Jessa. You and the baby." The word felt strange on his tongue.

But her smile was radiant—sleepy, but radiant.

He lay back, easing her into the circle of his arms. Her words spun in his head, fighting the peace and fulfillment her presence provided. He placed her hand over his heart and nudged her head forward onto his chest. "I love you, Jessa."

She peered up at him. "No regrets?"

"No regrets," he murmured, closing his eyes.

He pretended to sleep, his arms preventing her from rolling away this time. He felt it the minute she dropped off, going limp and soft against him. Her breath fanned across his bare chest, her fingers twitching sporadically, and her leg shifted, resting across his thighs. And even though he and his wolf were pleased she was sleeping peacefully, they were both sick with worry over the answers tomorrow would bring. Was this pregnancy a risk?

He'd lied to her, he had one regret. Not ripping out Cyrus's throat. Yes, the bastard was running scared, that was a start. But killing Cyrus was the only way he'd ever truly find peace.

Chapter Seventeen

Jessa ran her finger up the center of Finn's chest, tracing the crosscross scratches and deeper gouges. Were those teeth marks? He was covered in battle-wounds, probably as sore as she was—or worse. But that didn't ease the hunger that woke her.

The craving she had for this man never failed to astound her. But why now, when they were both bone-weary and grieving? How was it possible to yearn for his touch, ache for the press of his body, the hard thrust of him inside her? The answers weren't important. Only action. She leaned over him, her leg lifting off his.

His eyes popped open. "Jessa?"

She smiled down at him, a little guilty and more than a little aroused by the smile that creased the corner of his eyes. "Good morning."

He reached up, twining his hands in her hair. "It is every time I wake to see you in my arms."

The roughened skin of his palm caressed her cheek tenderly, almost reverently. She bent, tracing his wounds before pressing light kisses against them. "You look like you've been chewed up and spit out."

"Sort of." He rumbled deliciously. His blue eyes locked with hers, searching her face curiously.

"Finn," she managed, her breathing accelerating. "Love me." She pressed his hand to her breast. She traced his thumb against her nipple, arching into the stroke with a shudder. "Please."

He moved over her, smoothing her hair from her face. His hand continued what she wanted. And when she moaned, he stooped, sucking the tight peak of her breast into his mouth.

This was what she craved, what her body desired. She parted her legs, blushing at the smile he gave her.

"You make me so hard I hurt, Jessa." His words were rough, rolling over every nerve. "You're beautiful. So, damn beautiful." His hand slid up the inside of her thigh, the blade of her hip, the dimple of her belly-button, and up between her breasts. Her heart was thundering when he cupped her breast and bent to suck her deep into his mouth. His teeth grazed the edge of her pebbled nipple, pulling a whimper from deep inside her. He rested his head on her breast, watching his hand slide across the plain of her belly.

When his fingertips traced the inside of her thigh, she parted her legs for him.

She was ready for him, throbbing against the pads of his fingertips. Each stroke of the tight nub of her core had her body tightening and arching toward him. His thumb moved while he slid a long finger slowly inside.

He groaned against her thigh, setting a deep rhythm that had her writhing against him.

She turned into her pillow, muffling the sounds she was making. He threw the pillow across the room and cradled her close, holding her tight against him, chest to chest, hip to hip, his hand never stopping.

"I want to hear you," he growled out.

"Finn, please." Her hand slipped between them, clasping his wrist.

"Hold on to me," he rasped, adding a second finger, the rhythm of his thumb frantically working her tight nub.

He kissed her then, the seal of his lips catching her hoarse cries. She came apart in his hold, his whispered, "I love you," echoing in her ears.

"Finn." She felt him, hard and throbbing against her stomach. Her hands slid along his back, gripping his hips in invitation. He'd given her pleasure but she wanted more.

He slid deep with one thrust, his groan broken.

She cried out, struggling with the force of their passion. He made her feel alive, wanted, and cherished. And, looking in his eyes, his love for her was undeniable. Slow, sweet, deep strokes that reminded her she was his. That he was hers.

He was careful with her, teasing the fire that threatened to consume her. He watched her closely, studying her reactions. The friction built, each soft caress, feather-light stroke of his fingertip, pushing her closer to the edge.

"I love you," he said, his rhythm never changing.

She was lost then, pleasure crashed into her, sweeping her away in rush of sensation.

He followed, kissing her as his body jerked forward. He arched into her, his head thrown, and his moan echoing. He slumped over her, breathing hard and feeling deliciously heavy. She closed her eyes, running her hands up and down his back slowly.

He moved to her side so quickly, Jessa frowned.

But then his hand rested against her stomach. "Don't want to hurt you."

She lay there, all the worry and concern from the night before seeping back. Thomas's face. He'd believed what he'd told her, believed she was in danger. But how could that be true? She felt good, even battered and bruised. Maybe it was just the Others? If they hadn't had a baby in decades, as Ellen said, they would want to study her and this pregnancy? Unless Ellen wasn't hoping to save her, just her baby. She swallowed, hating the questions, the anxiety, that consumed her. She covered Finn's hand, needing comfort.

His thumb brushed across her knuckles.

"I miss Oscar," she murmured.

Finn smiled. "Me too. We'll meet them at the refuge later."

She sat up then, stretching. "Then let's hurry." She paused. "Except all I have is a hospital gown." She glanced at him over her shoulder, loving the hunger in his eyes as he stared at her bare back.

He ran a finger down her spine, crawling forward to press a kiss to the base of her back. She shuddered as his tongue and lips worked up her spine, latching onto the nape of her neck and sucking lightly.

His arms came around her, his fingers sliding up her breasts so his hands could cup them. He groaned, biting her neck gently. "The clothes can wait."

She closed her eyes and leaned into him, his hands were magic, working her nipples into tight peaks before sliding down her stomach and between her legs. Jessa gripped his thighs, the stroke of his thumb all that mattered. She was coming in seconds. His big hands pressed against her back, urging her onto her knees.

His fingers ran down her back, bracing her hips, and sank home.

She clenched, the girth of his arousal running against every nerve.

The sound he made was amazing. Guttural, raw, and hungry. She arched into him, his frenzy, the grip and slide of his hands, almost desperate. He pummeled into her and she tilted forward, welcoming all of him.

He lost it then. A broken curse, his fingers digging into her hips, as he folded over her. He growled out his climax, muffling the sound against her back.

He fell to his side, tucking her close. "Sorry," he panted.

She shook her head, unable to speak.

They lay there until breathing was easier.

"I'm going to shower. Join me?" Finn asked, nuzzling the back of her neck.

Jessa sighed, still tingling. "Give me a minute," she looked over her shoulder. "Not sure my legs will work yet."

"I'll get the water going." He pressed a kiss on her shoulder, the cold air against her skin signaling he was gone.

She curled up tightly, tugging the blanket over her, clinging to the warmth and security Finn inspired.

It faded quickly. The questions and fears that seemed manageable with him nearby turned impossibly overwhelming in his absence. Part of it was his confidence. He knew this world, had lived it. For Jessa, things were still equal parts fairy tale and nightmare.

Right now, she should hold on to the fairy tale. She had Finn. She had Oscar, sweet baby boy. Her family was safe. Why was she letting a lie eat away at the contentment she had every right to?

She stared up at the ceiling, resting her hands on her stomach. Finn said they'd find out when they saw Hollis. But she wanted to talk to Ellen.

It didn't take long for her to tug on a hotel bathrobe, write Finn a quick note, and head down the hall to Ellen's room, ignoring the odd looks she got en route. She knocked on the door firmly. "It's Jessa," she said.

The door opened immediately, Gentry's eyes widening. "Where's Finn?"

"Showering," she said, brushing past him and into the room.

Ellen sat on the bed, wearing an identical robe. She smiled at Jessa. "We could start a cult. Matching duds. All white. At least we'd be comfortable."

Jessa sat on the end of the bed. "How are you feeling?"

"Not bad. I'd have slept easier without all the noises and odors these two made," she glared at Dante and Gentry. "But my arm's better. I feel good." She glanced at Jessa, her smile fading. "You're keeping me?"

Jessa frowned. "You saved me. I couldn't leave you there."

Ellen nodded. "And I thank you for that."

"But?" Jessa probed.

"But I want to go home," she said. "To my pack."

"Not that there's much left but a large patch of scorched earth," Gentry said, sipping coffee. "You'd have been part of that barbecue."

"That place wasn't my home." Ellen frowned, her hands clenching in her lap.

"Where is home?" Jessa asked.

Ellen looked at her. "That's not really any of your business." She wasn't hostile, just matter-of-fact. "Will you let me go?"

Jessa looked at Dante. Clearly, that wasn't going to happen. He stood, all but barring the door, his arms crossed over his chest. She didn't know what had been said or decided as far as Ellen was concerned. She was with the Others, someone the pack listened to. It made sense to question her, to glean any information she might have before they freed her.

But the idea of holding Ellen captive—Jessa's stomach churned. She swallowed, pressing a hand to her belly.

Ellen smiled. "Ah, the joys of breeding."

Jessa's smile was thin, the threat of throwing up very real.

"She needs water," Ellen said to Dante.

Dante sighed, glared at Ellen, and did as she said.

The water helped. A little.

"Thank you," Jessa said. "You have children."

The pain in Ellen's eyes was unbearable. "No."

Jessa studied her, willing to beg for what she wanted. "Ellen, I need your help. Please. I'd like to think you're wrong, that I'm fine. That I won't die. But I don't want this baby to die. I think you can help me, help the baby." She sucked in a deep breath, fighting off tears. "I'm begging you to stay. After that, I give you my word you're free to go."

Ellen's eyes blinked in surprise. She hesitated, chewing on her thumbnail and studying Jessa for what seemed like an eternity. Finally, she slid forward, pressing her hand against Jessa's stomach. She sighed, her rigid posture—her fight—fading before Jessa's eyes.

"For the baby, Jessa." Ellen looked at her, her gaze hard. "Not for you. Not for him. He is my enemy. You all are. But for the survival of our kind, I will help you."

Jessa smiled. "Thank you Ellen. Thank you." She clasped Ellen's hand in hers, squeezing it softly. Her gaze fell, noting the scars that wrapped around her forearms. Some old, white and thickened, others new—not quite healed. Ellen yanked her hand away, making Gentry leap to his feet and Dante tower over them both.

Ellen leaned back against the headboard, smiling.

But Jessa saw the way the woman's gaze darted nervously around the room. She pulled her hands into her robe. But it didn't cover her neck. And Jessa saw just as many scars there.

The pounding on the door made them all jump.

"Open the fucking door now," Finn's growl.

Dante opened the door. "Morning to you, too."

But Finn was staring at Jessa, his expression almost haunted as he crossed the room and tugged her onto her feet. "Don't ever do that again."

"What—"

"Cyrus is still out there Jessa," Finn spoke carefully, his

rage barely in check. "Without one of us at your side, I can't protect you. Don't. Ever. Do. That. Again."

Jessa saw through his anger. Fear rolled off him. Fear for her. Because she'd been so caught up in what she needed she hadn't stopped to think it through. He was right. Cyrus was out there. So was Byron. And if the farm wasn't Ellen's home, that meant there were more places the Others lived. More places and, likely, more Others.

"I won't, I promise." She slid her arms around his waist. "I'm sorry."

• • •

Finn stood under the water, waiting and waiting... Until he knew something wasn't right. She wasn't in the room. And his wolf came undone. Not that he could go tearing around the hotel as a goddamn wolf. He'd tugged on his sweats and run, hoping he'd catch her scent and follow her. It was surprisingly easy. While he'd been worst-casing things, she'd headed straight to the other room. To Ellen. For answers, of course.

He'd leaned against the door, hair wet, shirtless, causing the hotel patrons to smile and whisper as they passed by. But he had to get a grip before he went into the room, had to rein in the urge to fight. There was nothing to fight. Only fear.

They had enough things to fear without his mind getting the best of him. Having Jessa back in his arms helped. But it didn't erase the very real threats out there.

He hoped Hollis's investigation would reveal Cara's cause of death was the car accident. If not–they'd figure it out.

And Cyrus was loose. But the great alpha was afraid and, for the most part, alone. It would take time for him to rally reinforcements. Time Finn would use to learn everything he could about the Others.

Ellen was the key to that.

After they'd boarded the jet he'd charted to Montana, after Jessa had fallen asleep, he crept to the back of the plane to hash things out.

"What's the plan?" Dante asked.

Finn glanced at Ellen.

Dante nodded.

"I can't communicate telepathically with my pack so say what you want. I gave your mate my word. I keep my word." She wouldn't look at him, she had yet to make any eye contact with him. But he believed her.

"What, exactly, did you agree to?" he asked.

"To help with the whole pregnancy thing," Dante muttered. "Is Jessa in danger?" his voice lowered.

"I don't know—"

"Yes," Ellen shifted.

Finn glared at her. "You know this because?"

Ellen shook her head. "My deal is with her. Not you."

Finn sighed, running a hand through his hair. "We're going to strike a separate deal." He sat in front of her, staring at her.

She smiled, looking at her hands. "No thank you." He heard the snap to her voice, her wolf responding to his order.

But she wasn't his pack. Was she? Could he make her obey him? Finn gritted his teeth, his wolf desperate to show her who was in charge. "I'm not asking."

"Maybe we should wait until we land to get under each other's skin?" Gentry asked, nervous. "Wolves in the sky— not something I'm equipped to handle."

"Good call," Dante seconded.

Finn sat back, watching Ellen.

She looked confused. Her gaze shifted from Gentry to Dante, stealing a quick glance his way. "You're going to listen to them?" her question was tight.

Finn sighed. "I'd rather not. But, yes, I am." He stood, ignoring her. "We're heading to the refuge. Hollis can work best there. And, for now, it makes sense for us to be there. But if you need to go, I'll respect that," he looked at Dante. "I don't think Cyrus will try again for a while. He didn't like what he saw. We scared him. Which means, right now, we have the advantage."

Dante nodded. "Think I'll stay for a while."

"Yeah, me, too," Gentry added, grinning.

Finn chuckled, shaking his head at the man who'd risked everything for a paycheck. Whether Gentry was a wolf, he'd earned his place in the pack. He'd never force his pack to do something they didn't want to do. He wasn't Cyrus. But there was no denying the comfort and relief that having them together—united—provided. He felt stronger, braver, and more confident in himself and his wolf.

He had to believe that Hollis would have the answers they needed. And then, he'd find Cyrus and end this once and for all.

Chapter Eighteen

Oscar had grown.

"Good to see you, sis," Harry hugged her, placing Oscar in her arms. "Everything okay? I get the feeling there's a lot going on we're not supposed to know about."

She hugged Harry, hard. Could she tell him? How could she not? They were her family, now and always. Besides, there was no way she could keep her pregnancy a secret. "Not yet, okay? But soon, I promise."

"I'm not worried." Harry grinned. "You've never been able to keep a secret."

She sat, holding Oscar while Landon complained about school. Then Nate updated her on his progress in karate. They were happy, healthy, and here. It was the first time in a long, long time she felt at ease.

"Brown's taking us on a tour of the refuge," Nate said, slipping on his parka. "Said we might see some wolves."

"Don't worry." Landon nudged his little brother. "You're too scrawny to eat."

She laughed, waving them off before going to make a

bottle for Oscar.

For the time being, she wouldn't think about anything but this. Having him cradled close, his sweet smell, the sounds of him breathing in an otherwise quiet room, were enough. She'd missed him—missed this. Being his mom and nothing else. No worries or cares, only love and comfort.

She pressed kisses to the top of his head and lay him in his crib, covering him with a thick blanket and staring down at him. He stretched, his little mouth stretching wide and one foot poking out from under the covers.

"It's too cold," Jessa whispered, smoothing the blanket over Oscar and resting her hand on his stomach. "Sleep sweet."

"Okay?" Finn asked, his arms slipping around her waist.

She relaxed into him. "Better than okay."

"He missed you," Finn whispered against her ear.

"How do you know?" she rested her head on his shoulder and looked up at him.

"He's his father's son. Meaning he's only at ease when you're close."

She turned, her arms slipping up and around his neck. "This is where I want to be." She stroked the almost faded scratch on his cheek.

His gaze searched hers.

"What's wrong?" she asked.

"Nothing." He shook his head, tracing her features with his fingertips.

She stood on tiptoe, welcoming the touch of his lips on hers, the mingling of breath, and the slight tightening of his grip.

"You need to eat," he said, sliding from her hold and taking her hand.

She didn't argue. She was hungry. And now that they were safely at home, she had an appetite. Odd that she considered the refuge more of a home than his apartment. She was a Texas native, but this place was special.

Dante and Anders had gathered in the kitchen. Tension filled the room, threatening her appetite. If something else had happened, she didn't want to know. Not yet. She wanted to sit, eat, smile at them, and pretend like this was a normal family dinner. "Anyone hungry?" Jessa asked, opening the refrigerator to peer inside. "Something quick."

"I made stew," Anders offered. "Gallons of it. Big pot in the back."

"Perfect," Jessa said, pulling the massive stewpot forward and placing it on the cooktop. "I'll warm it up and make some biscuits."

Anders hopped up and started pulling supplies together while she turned on the oven. She glanced around the room.

Hollis emerged from his office, scanning the contents of a file as he crossed the room and went out the other side.

"When did Hollis get here?" she asked, smiling at Finn.

"A few hours ago," Finn said, smiling back.

"Good to see he's relaxing," she teased.

But Finn's smile tightened. She frowned at him, glancing after Hollis. "Where's Ellen?" she asked.

Dante cleared his throat, "Hollis is talking to her. We're keeping her in one of the secure—"

"No," Jessa slapped her wooden spoon the lip of the bowl. "She's not a prisoner. Finn, she gave me her word she'd help me. For crying out loud, she saved my life. I think a little trust isn't asking too much."

"Trust her? So, she can hurt you? Or Oscar?" Finn ran his fingers through his hair, a sure sign of his agitation. "Dammit, Jessa, I just got you back. I'm not putting you at risk."

"She has something to gain from this." Jessa paused, drawing all eyes on her. "She said there had been no pups—babies—born in years. She thinks I, this pregnancy, might help her understand why."

"So Cyrus and his pack can make more of their kind?" Dante snapped.

"Their kind?" Ellen's voice was low, pausing just inside the kitchen, Hollis close behind. "Are we not the same?" she asked, glancing around the room. "Our hatred is mutual, no need to pretend otherwise. But the mate is right. My pack suffers cruelly."

"Please, sit." Hollis walked around her and pulled a chair out at the table. "Civility is the only chance we stand of a successful collaboration. Let's try?"

She sat, stiffly, nodding at Hollis.

"How are you feeling Ellen?" Jessa asked, rolling out the dough.

Ellen nodded again.

"Hungry?" she asked.

Ellen looked at her, her mismatched eyes intent as they regarded her. "Did you tell her?" she asked, glancing at Hollis.

Hollis shook his head. "No. I was waiting for the opportune time. Which, apparently, is now."

"I see no point delaying," Ellen said. "We have four months before—"

"Fine," Hollis interrupted. "Cara's death was expedited by the car accident. But she would have died before Oscar was born. And, chances are, Oscar would have died as well."

"Four months?" Finn asked.

"Wolves gestate for two months. Humans for nine. Werewolves fall somewhere in the middle," Ellen explained, sounding bored.

That explained why the pregnancy test showed positive so early—and why she was already experiencing symptoms. But not much time. Jessa stopped rolling the dough, the roller suddenly too heavy to move.

"I got this Jessa," Anders took the rolling pin.

"Four months?" Finn repeated.

"Jesus," Dante groaned, covering his face.

Finn was at her side, his arm wrapped around her waist. His feather-light kiss, against her temple, calmed her. But she still relied on him to guide her to a chair at the table. He sat next to her, capturing her hand in his.

"Cara was seeing a hematologist, often. They had no idea what was going on, noting everything from a possible rare infection she'd picked up on an international shoot to alcoholism or, possibly, prolonged narcotics use. Everything was a stretch, but the doctor did try, I'll give him that. It looks like she had several blood transfusions. Then, because of the constant increase in kidney function, her kidneys began to fail so they tried a form of dialysis, to clean the blood. She seemed to improve initially, but—" he paused, tapping the file he'd been reading. "But the further along, the more blood, the more waste in her system. Without those enzymes and proteins being absorbed, they'd be recycled to the baby. And they'd grow weaker, sicker until…" He shook his head. "The crash was probably the only thing that saved Oscar."

Jessa listened, horrified. That poor woman. She'd suffered, unknowing, fighting to bring her baby into the world.

"You can fix it?" Finn question was flat. "Tell me you can fix it."

"Yes," Ellen spoke quickly, smiling at Jessa. "But we don't agree on the answer."

"Why?" Finn asked, agitated.

Hollis's focused only on Finn. "I'm a scientist, Finn, you know that. I study, analyze, dissect, and know before I do a goddamn thing. Her idea is—"

"The only way to ensure she'll live. That the baby will live." Ellen sat back in her chair, crossing her arms over her chest.

Finn's hand tightened on Jessa's. Hollis focused on his

hands, closing around hers. Warm, strong, secure. She drew in a deep breath.

"What are the ideas?" she asked. "I'd like to know my options."

"Termination," Hollis said. "That would be the easiest option."

Ellen growled.

Jessa swallowed, glancing at Finn. He was staring at the table, his jaw clenched, everything about him rigid.

"The transfusions were right. The blood was wrong. Wolf's blood, your blood, Finn. Ellen and I agree on that. Your blood is the key to the bloodline."

"Won't that affect Jessa?" Finn asked. "Won't that turn her?"

"Not while she's pregnant," Hollis said.

"A werewolf doesn't shift when she's pregnant," Ellen explained. "Too dangerous for the pup. Full moons are hard, fever, nausea, weakness—but not change."

"Sounds like you, Hollis," Anders tried to tease.

Everyone stared at him.

"The dialysis was also sound," Hollis said. "Cleaning the blood of impurities, preventing her body from getting toxic. But the last few weeks I'd recommend she remain connected to the machine—"

Finn released her, standing and crossing the room. He ran a hand through his hair then over his face.

"She'll be alive," Hollis added.

"Or you bite her," Ellen. "Turn her now and never worry over her again."

Jessa stared at Ellen, at the certainty in the woman's eyes. She believed what she said.

"And the risk that the change would end the pregnancy?" Hollis asked. "If the pack hasn't been able to breed, why would this be different?"

Ellen opened her mouth, looked at Finn, and closed it again. She sat back, shrugging. "It is."

"What if you're both wrong?" Finn asked. "What if — "

"What if the reason Cara was sick was because she wasn't his mate?" Jessa asked. She knew Finn belonged to her. Their connection was irrefutable. Why wouldn't that extend to a visible bond—healthy children? "Ellen, the women in your pack, the women that lost babies, were they mated? Or, pets, I believe they called them?"

Ellen frowned. "Some. I think."

Hollis was studying her. "A relevant point, Jessa."

Ellen nodded. "Maybe. Could it be so simple?"

Hollis grinned at her before looking at Ellen, excited. "Can you make a list? Names and anything relevant, if they were mates? To test your theory."

"Yes, yes," Ellen waved her hand at Hollis. "But don't put me in the basement."

"No," Finn agreed. "You are our guest. Until you prove otherwise."

Jessa smiled at him, mouthing, *Thank you.*

• • •

Jessa's excitement was a thing of wonder. Finn's heart, his body, responded immediately. He loved her so completely he could not, would not, lose her.

"Odds?" Finn asked, his gaze fixed on her.

Her green eyes met his.

"I… I don't know," Hollis said. "She bears your mark. She is your mate, part of you. Cara wasn't. Ellen and I need to do some digging, I think. But I have no guarantee."

"There are never any guarantees," Ellen said. "Time will tell."

"If she gets sick?" Dante asked.

"We move forward with treatment," Hollis said.

"Or you infect her," Ellen offered.

"Or I don't get sick," Jessa said, smiling at him. "What have we got to lose?"

Everything. But Finn kept his mouth shut. If Hollis's idea didn't work, then he'd consider Ellen's. He'd never thought to turn her. She deserved better. But she wanted this family. And, selfish bastard that he was, he would do whatever he had to keep her. Even turn her… If that's what she wanted.

Hollis and Ellen seemed pacified. Jessa, amazingly serene. He wanted that. Wanted her peace.

"Food's ready," Anders called out.

Finn watched the rest of the kitchen come alive, as if the previous conversation hadn't torn him to pieces.

"Eat," Jessa said, offering him a bowl of stew.

He took the bowl from her and set it on the mantel next to him. He cupped her head, tilting her toward him so he could see all of her.

She stared up at him.

He took her hand and led her from the room, down the hall, and into their bedroom. He let go of her, pacing from the fireplace to Oscar's crib. His son, sleeping peacefully, content. "I'm scared," he whispered.

She stepped close, taking his hand in hers. "Don't be. I'm right. We'll be fine." She seemed so right. He wanted her to be. "You trust us? You trust our bond?"

He nodded.

"Then trust me. Try," her tone was soft, entreating. "I feel it, Finn. As strong as our bond."

"I will." He stared down at her, searching for the right words.

"But?"

"I've lived the last ten years giving a shit about nothing. Nothing, Jessa. I did what I was supposed to, followed through on my responsibilities, went through the motions. My wolf was as much my enemy as the Others, something I resented. A curse. One I'd forced on those I valued most." He paused. "Now I have you. And I realize how desperate I am to keep you. If it's the only way, I'll turn you—for me. Because I can't give you up."

"You won't have to." She hugged him, pressing her cheek against his chest. "Cyrus said the bond didn't count because I wasn't a wolf but I—"

Finn's held her tightly, needing the pump of her heart and the thrum of her pulse. "I should have killed him."

"Finn—"

"I will kill him," he said, burying his nose in her hair. "My family won't live in fear of him."

"I'm pretty sure he's the one that's afraid now," she said, looking up at him. "From what I saw, you were terrifyingly efficient. There were so many."

"I was lost. I thought I'd lost you. All I cared about was getting even."

She frowned. "No matter what, you have to be here for our son. Oscar needs you, Finn. You have to be there for him."

"I need you," he whispered, fighting the lingering fear of losing her. "I always will."

"I'm not going anywhere." She ran her fingers through her hair. "Women have babies all the time. I'm not worried. So, you can't be. You're my mate. My partner. My alpha." Her hands slid along his neck to his shoulders. "My lover."

He nodded. "Your husband."

Her eyes widened. "Is that a proposal? It sort of sounded like an—"

"Order," he finished. "I'm not asking. I told you that night, once you agreed to be my mate, I'd never let you go."

"The bond isn't enough?" she asked.

"For me, yes. But it might be best for the rest of the world to know it too, so the wolf doesn't get angry." He pressed a lingering kiss to the corner of her mouth.

She smiled. "Then I'd better marry you. Even if you're not asking."

"He can get very protective when it comes to you." His hand slid through her hair, his want raging hot and heavy through his blood. "And possessive." His tongue brushed between her lips, drawing a gratifying gasp from her.

"Show me," she managed.

"Is that an order?' he asked, his hands fisting in her hair.

"Yes." She moaned as he sucked her earlobe into his mouth. "Always."

"Always," Finn agreed, he and his wolf happily giving her what she wanted.

About the Author

Sasha grew up surrounded by books. Her passions have always been storytelling, romance, history, and travel. Her first play was written for her Girl Scout troop. She's been writing ever since. She loves getting lost in the worlds and characters she creates; even if she frequently forgets to run the dishwasher or wash socks when she's doing so. Luckily, her four brilliant children and hero-inspiring hubby are super understanding and supportive.

Discover the Blood Moon Brotherhood series

RESCUED BY THE WOLF

PROTECTING THE WOLF'S MATE

Also by Sasha A. Summers

ACCIDENTALLY FAMILY

Discover more paranormal romance titles from Entangled...

WHEN DANGER BITES
a Bravo Team WOLF novel by Heather Long

Buttoned-up Corporal Kaitlyn Amador is dangerous on every level. Marine Captain Jax can survive the temptation for only so long before his wolf takes over and pursues what it wants.

DRAKON'S PLUNDER
a Blood of the Drakon novel by N.J. Walters

Archeologist Sam Bellamy doesn't believe in dragons, but the secret society called the Knights of the Dragon do, and if she can get one of the artifacts they're searching for away from them, she'll consider it payback for killing her mentor. Four-thousand-year-old water drakon Ezra Easton knows just because he pulled an injured woman from the ocean, doesn't mean he gets to keep her... When she wakes up, she has a tall tale to share, and it seems the Knights are after her. But this drakon won't give up his treasure.

LONE WOLFE PROTECTOR
a Wolfe Creek novel by Kaylie Newell

When Maggie Sullivan comes to Wolfe Creek, determined to find out why her best friend vanished one fog-shrouded night a year ago, seasoned sheriff's deputy Koda Wolfe reluctantly agrees to help. Soon he's compelled to protect Maggie from herself, his family's ancient curse, and a killer who could strike again. The nights heat up in more ways than one as Maggie and Koda begin a fiery relationship. But as they delve deeper into the disappearance, the eerie woods come alive with secrets bound to tear them apart. And someone is watching their every move.